W9-CDN-067

Hudson Area Public Library
Hudson, IL 61748

DISCARD

19.99

EDGAR ALLAN POE

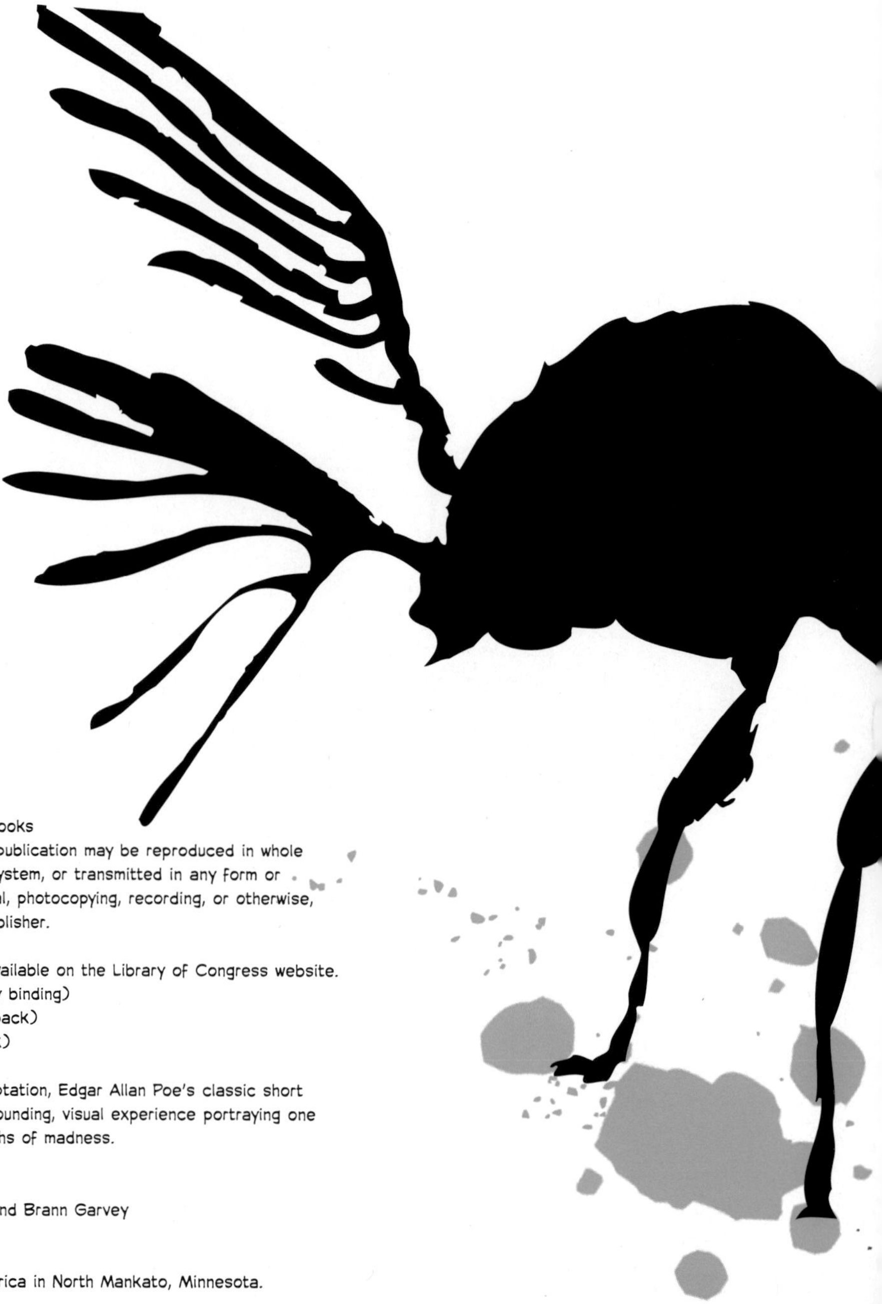

Edgar Allan Poe Graphic Novels
are published by Stone Arch Books
A Capstone Imprint
1710 Roe Crest Drive
North Mankato, MN 56003
www.capstonepub.com

Copyright © 2013 by Stone Arch Books
All rights reserved. No part of this publication may be reproduced in whole
or in part, or stored in a retrieval system, or transmitted in any form or
by any means, electronic, mechanical, photocopying, recording, or otherwise,
without written permission of the publisher.

Cataloging-in-Publication Data is available on the Library of Congress website.
ISBN: 978-1-4342-3023-2 (library binding)
ISBN: 978-1-4342-4261-7 (paperback)
ISBN: 978-1-4342-5964-6 (eBook)

Summary: In this graphic novel adaptation, Edgar Allan Poe's classic short
story is transformed into a heart-pounding, visual experience portraying one
man's journey into the dizzying depths of madness.

Art Director: Bob Lentz
Graphic Designers: Hilary Wacholz and Brann Garvey
Edited by: Sean Tulien

Printed in the United States of America in North Mankato, Minnesota.
092012   006933CGS13

THE TELL-TALE HEART

by EDGAR ALLAN POE
RETOLD by BENJAMIN HARPER
ILLUSTRATED by DENNIS CALERO

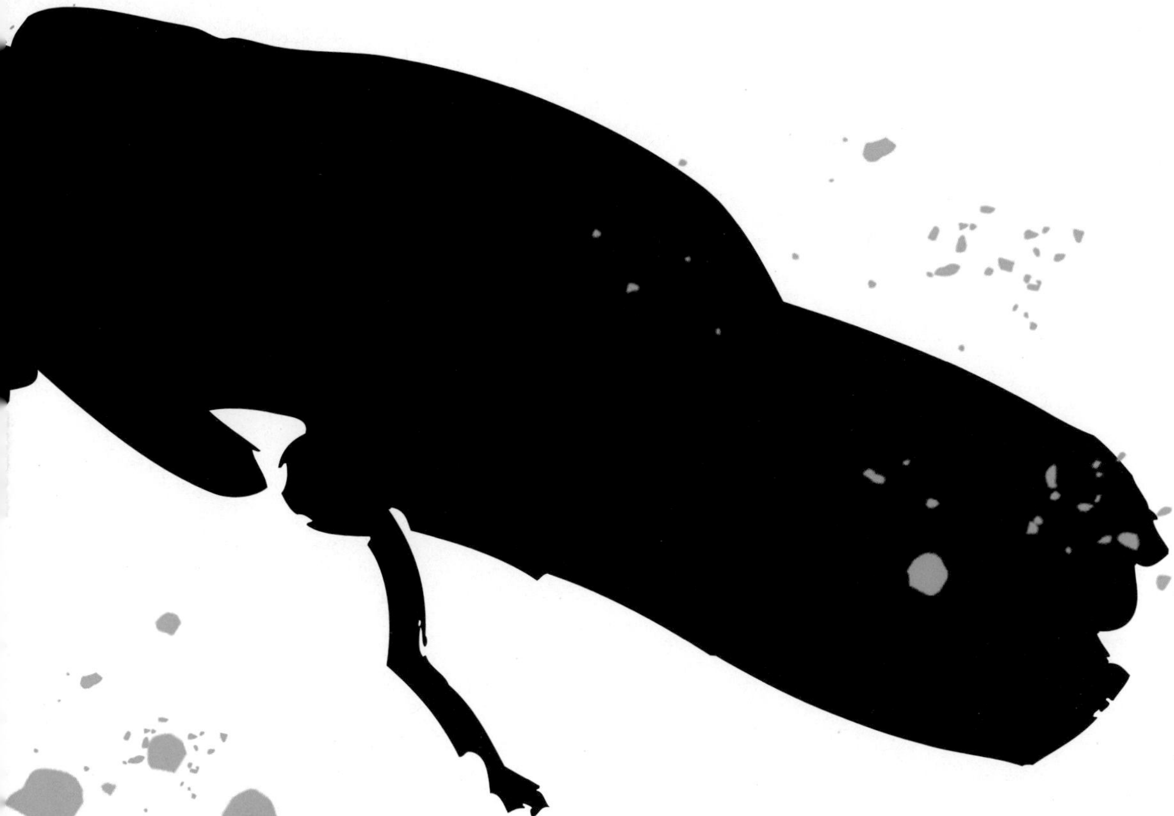

STONE ARCH BOOKS • A CAPSTONE IMPRINT

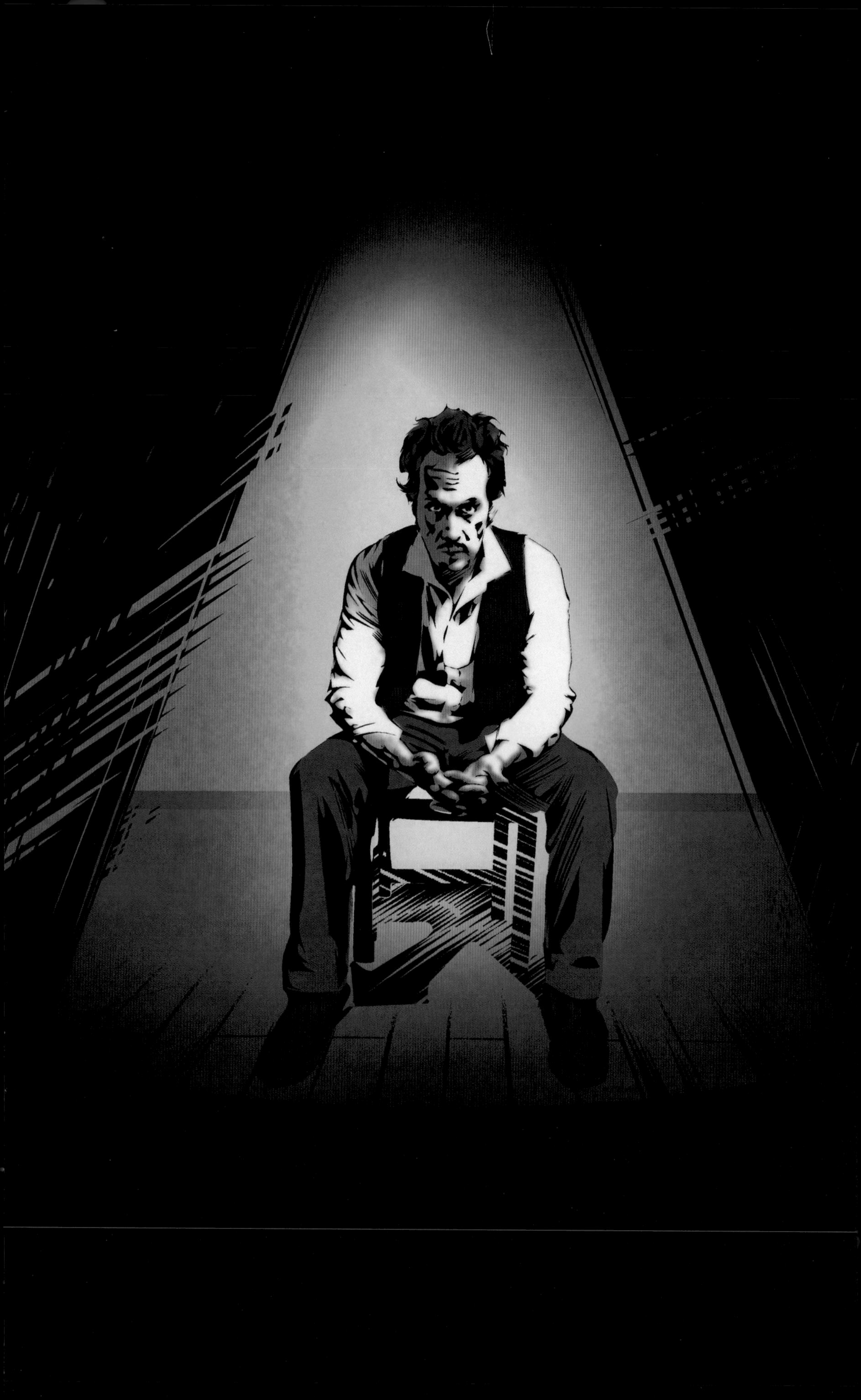

Art is long, and Time is fleeting,
And our hearts, though stout and brave,
Still, like muffled drums, are beating
Funeral marches to the grave.
– Longfellow

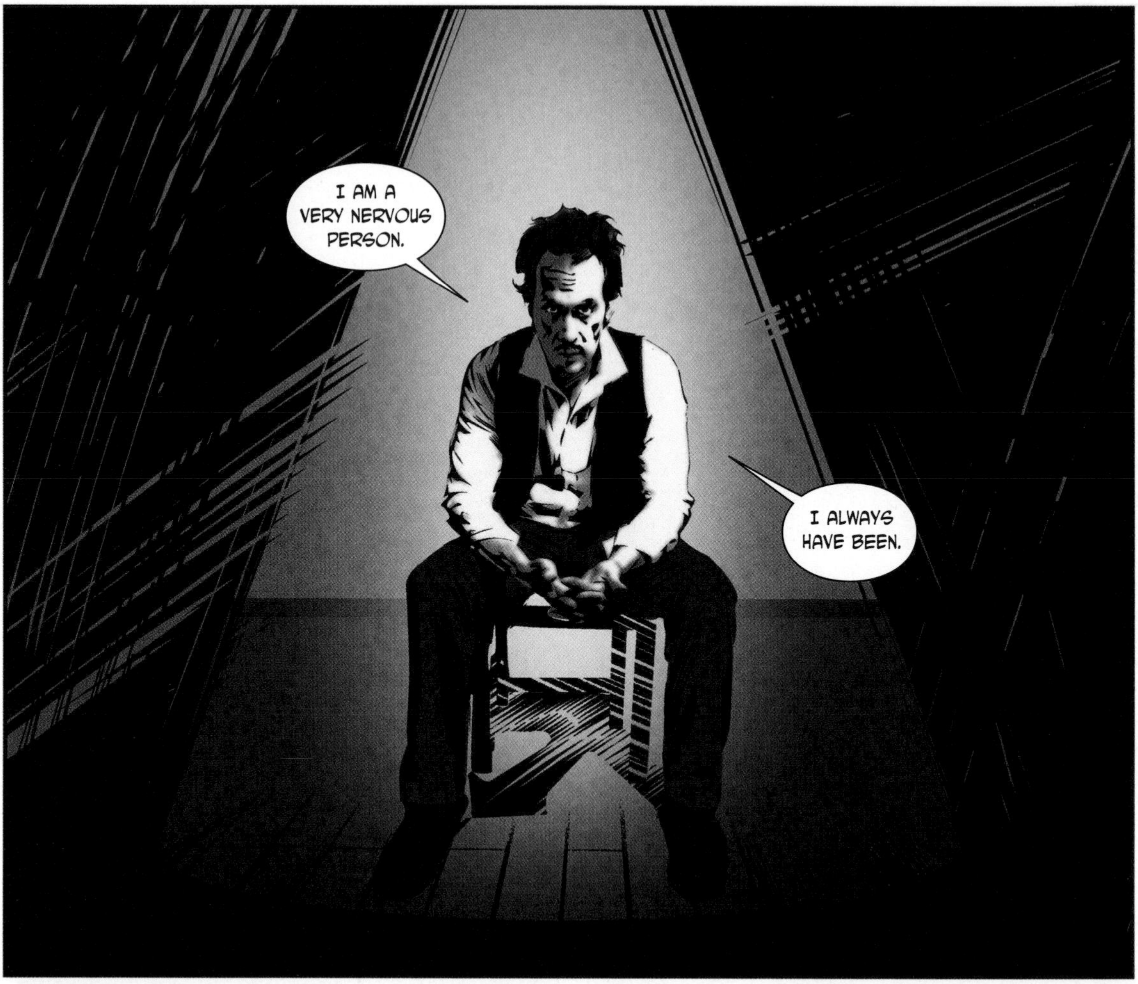
I AM A VERY NERVOUS PERSON.
I ALWAYS HAVE BEEN.

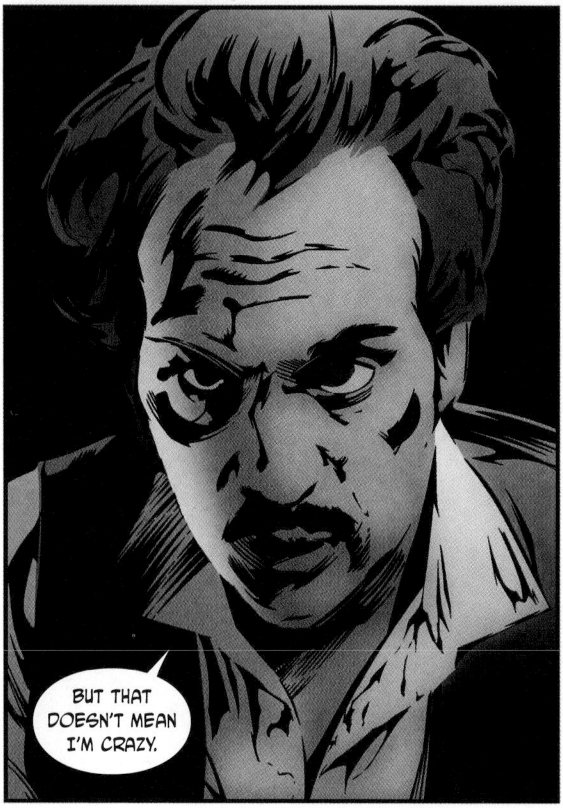
BUT THAT DOESN'T MEAN I'M CRAZY.

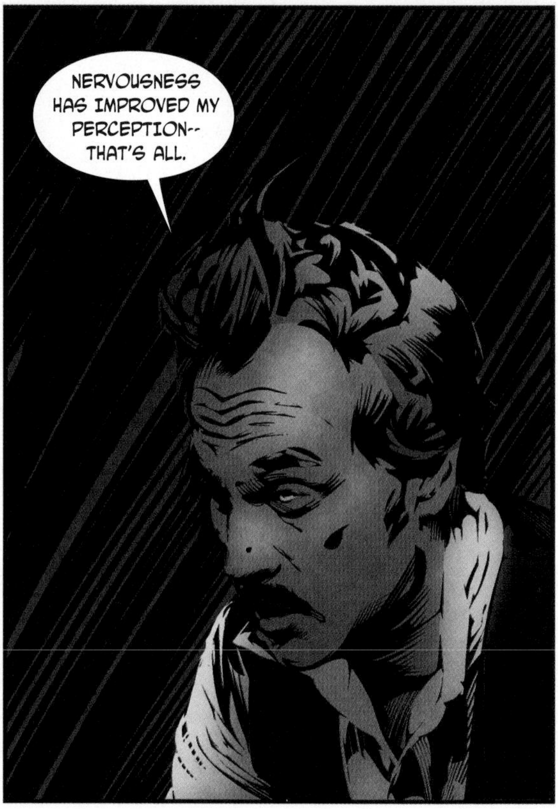
NERVOUSNESS HAS IMPROVED MY PERCEPTION-- THAT'S ALL.

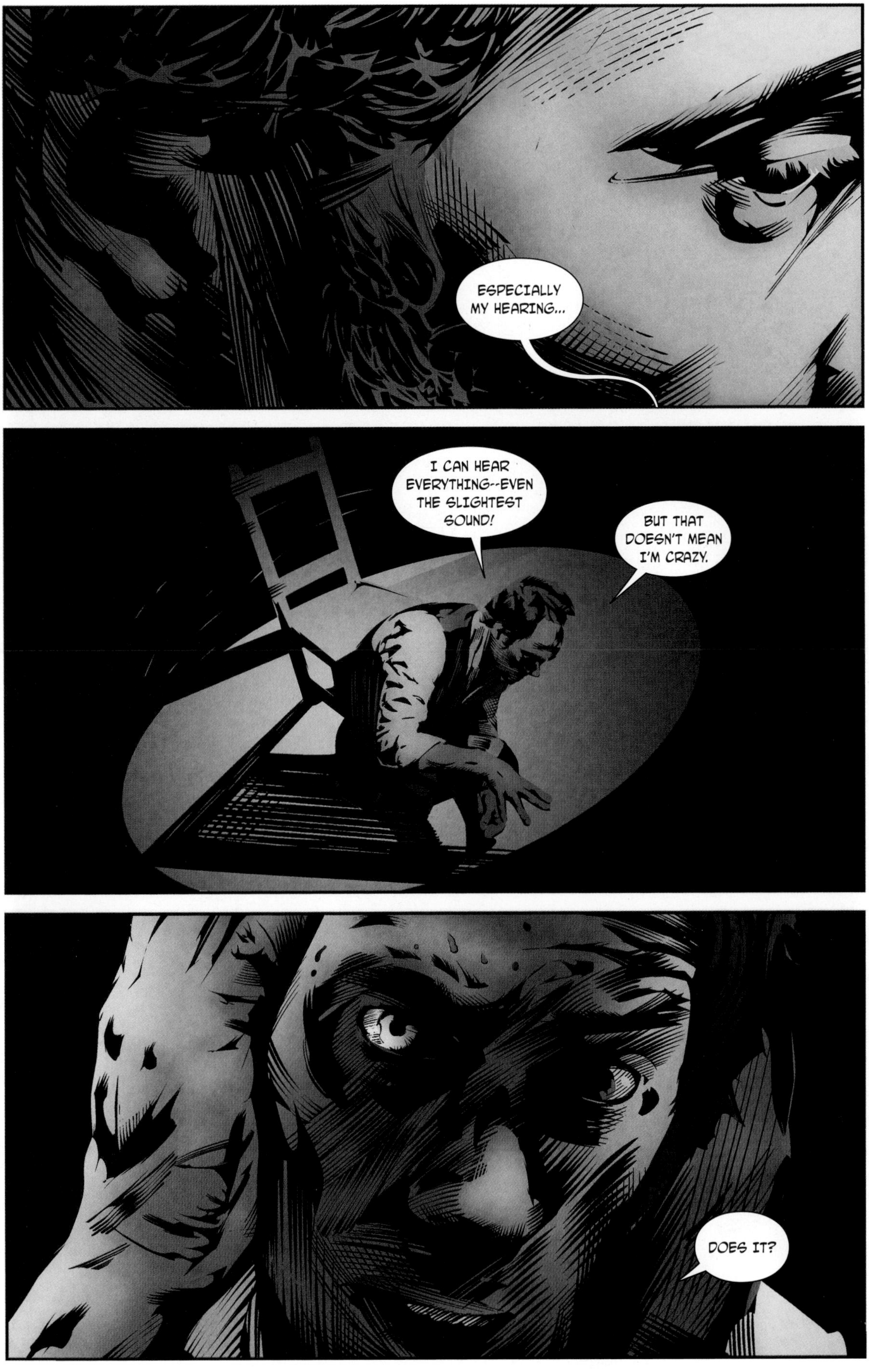
ESPECIALLY MY HEARING...
I CAN HEAR EVERYTHING--EVEN THE SLIGHTEST SOUND!
BUT THAT DOESN'T MEAN I'M CRAZY.
DOES IT?

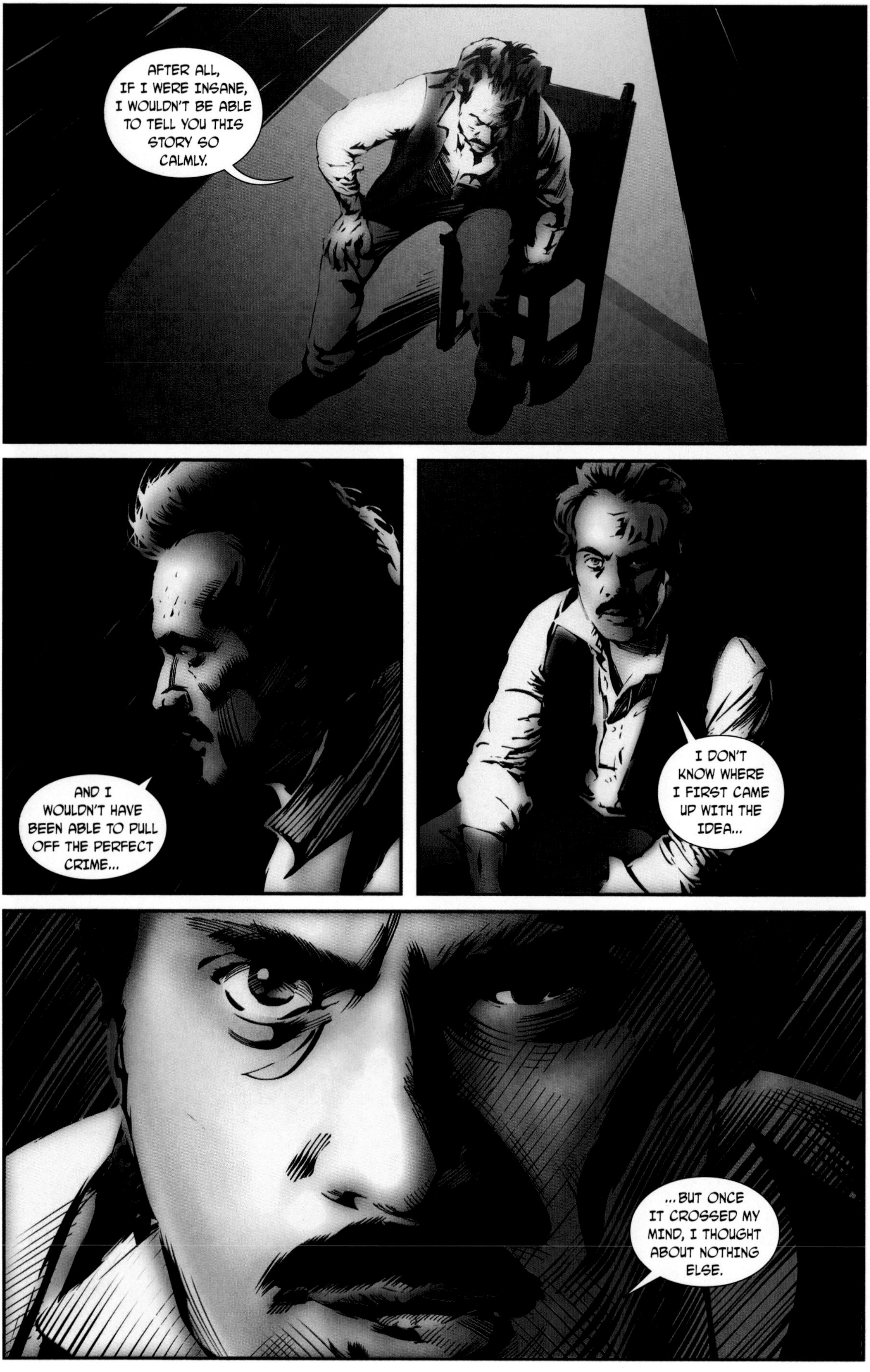
AFTER ALL, IF I WERE INSANE, I WOULDN'T BE ABLE TO TELL YOU THIS STORY SO CALMLY.
AND I WOULDN'T HAVE BEEN ABLE TO PULL OFF THE PERFECT CRIME...
I DON'T KNOW WHERE I FIRST CAME UP WITH THE IDEA...
...BUT ONCE IT CROSSED MY MIND, I THOUGHT ABOUT NOTHING ELSE.

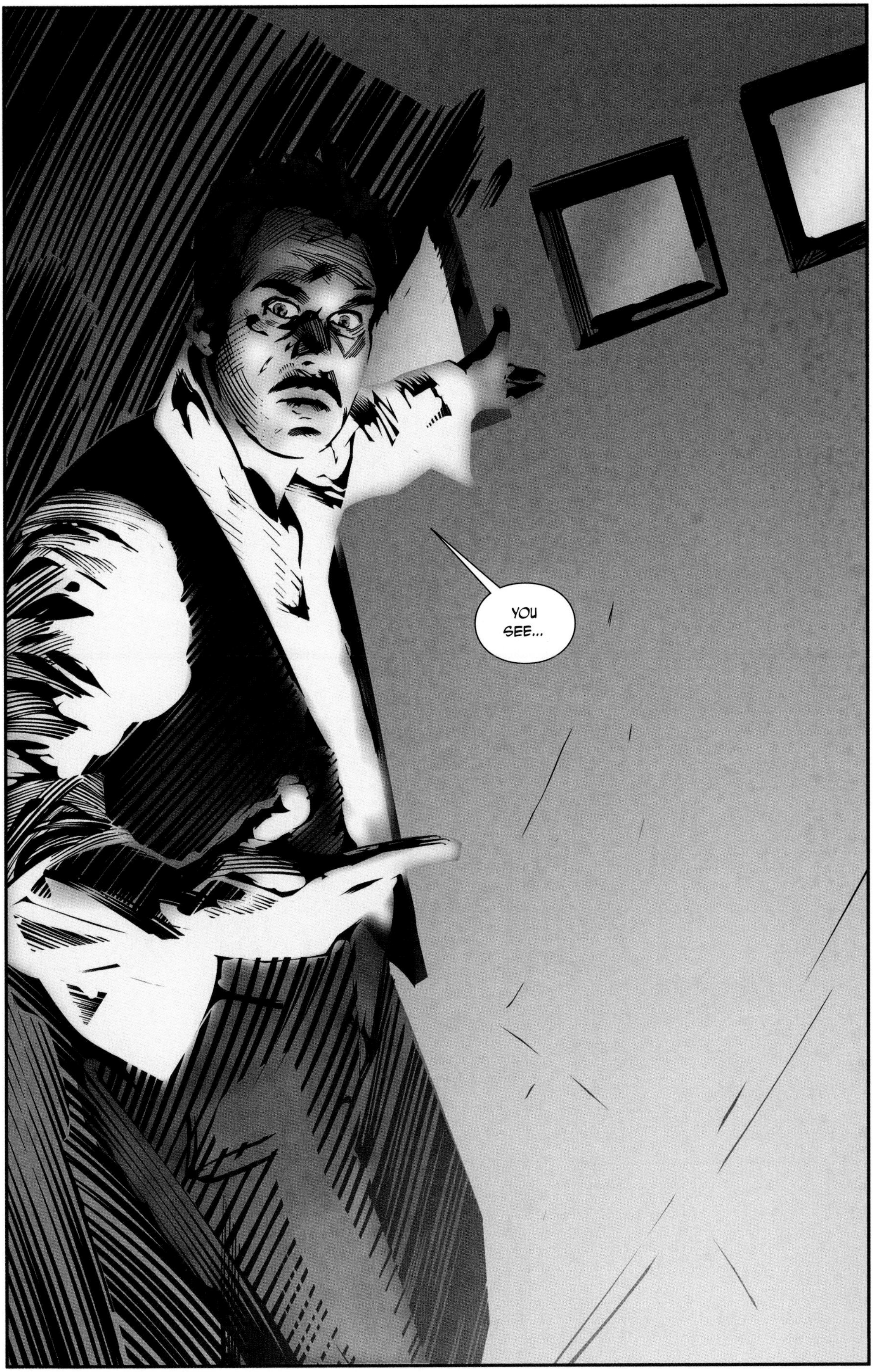
YOU
SEE...

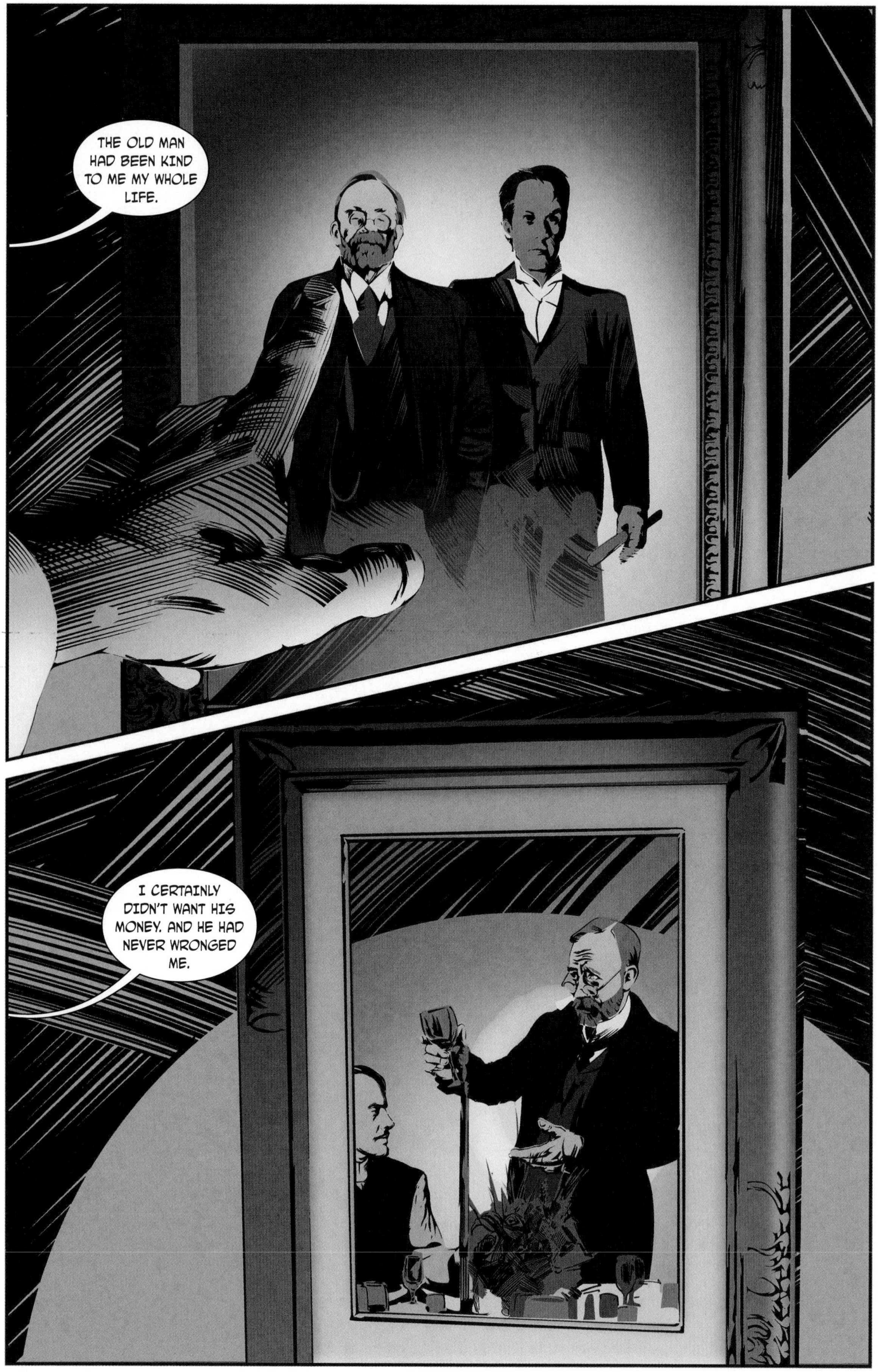
THE OLD MAN HAD BEEN KIND TO ME MY WHOLE LIFE.
I CERTAINLY DIDN'T WANT HIS MONEY. AND HE HAD NEVER WRONGED ME.

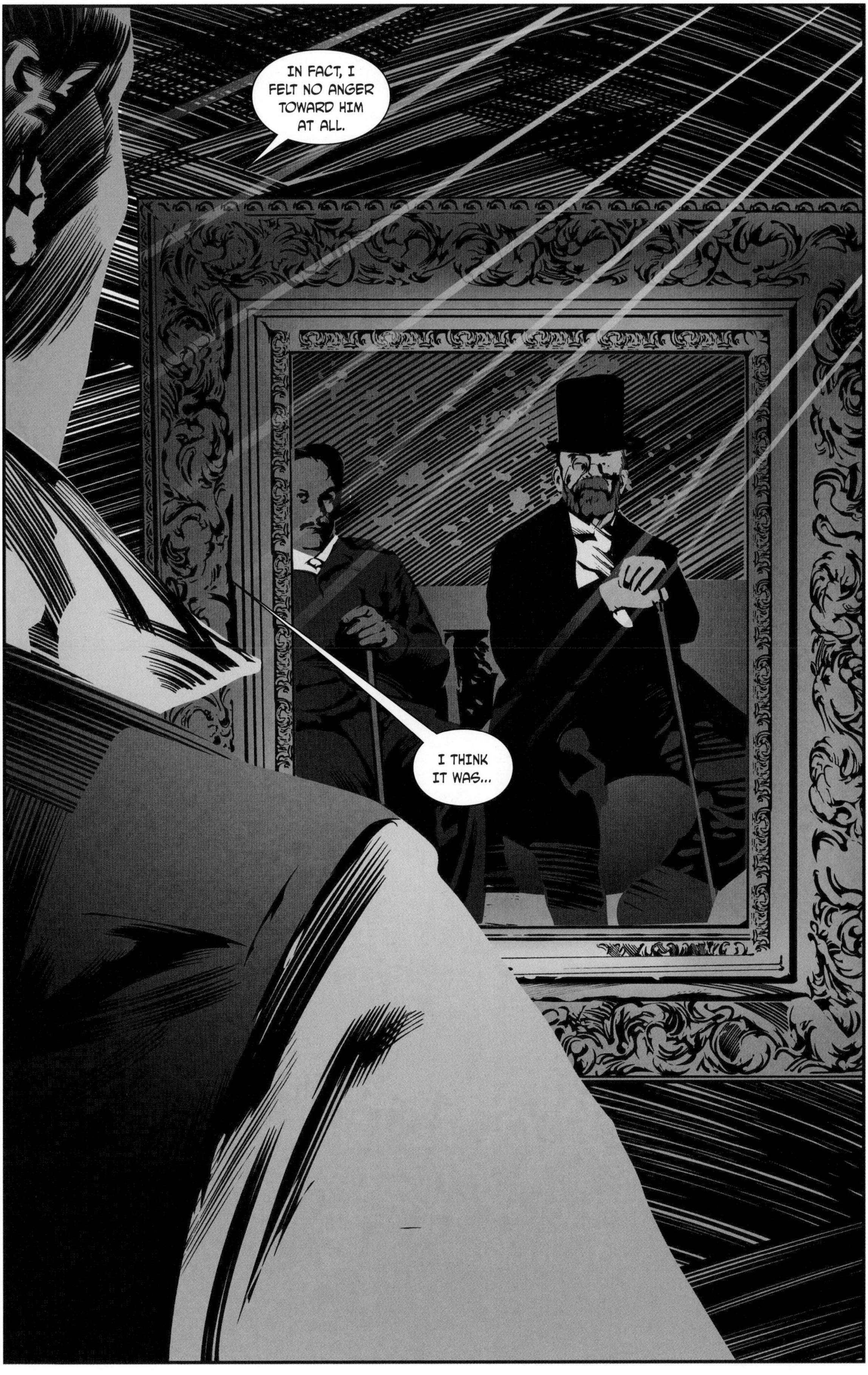
IN FACT, I FELT NO ANGER TOWARD HIM AT ALL.
I THINK IT WAS...

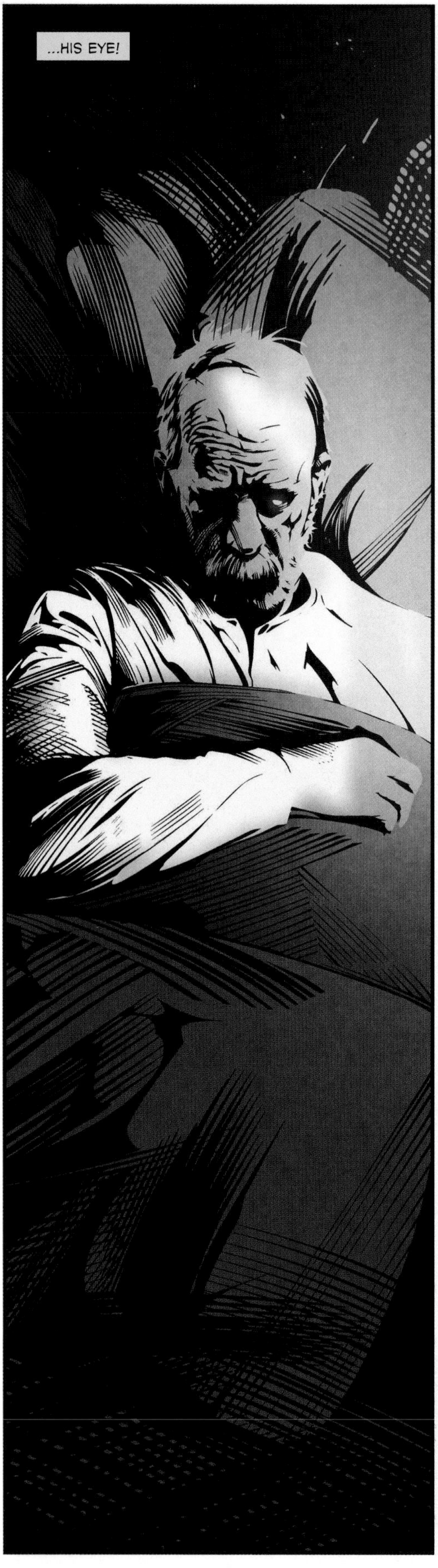
...HIS EYE!

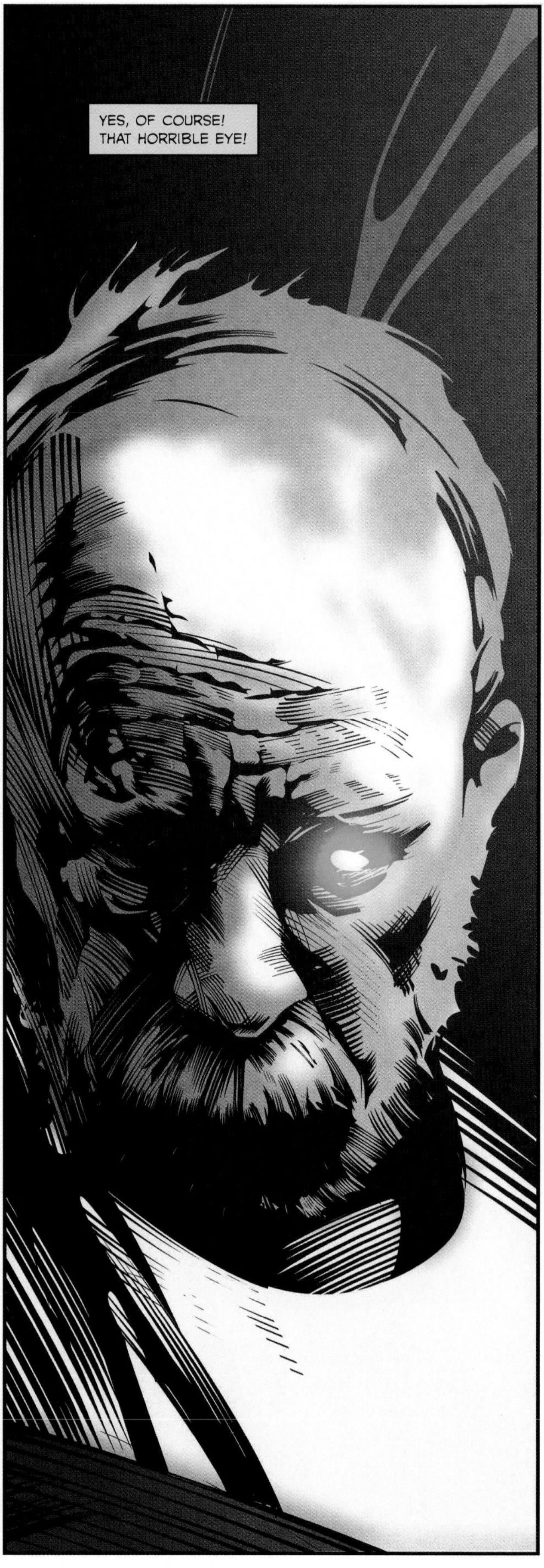
YES, OF COURSE!
THAT HORRIBLE EYE!

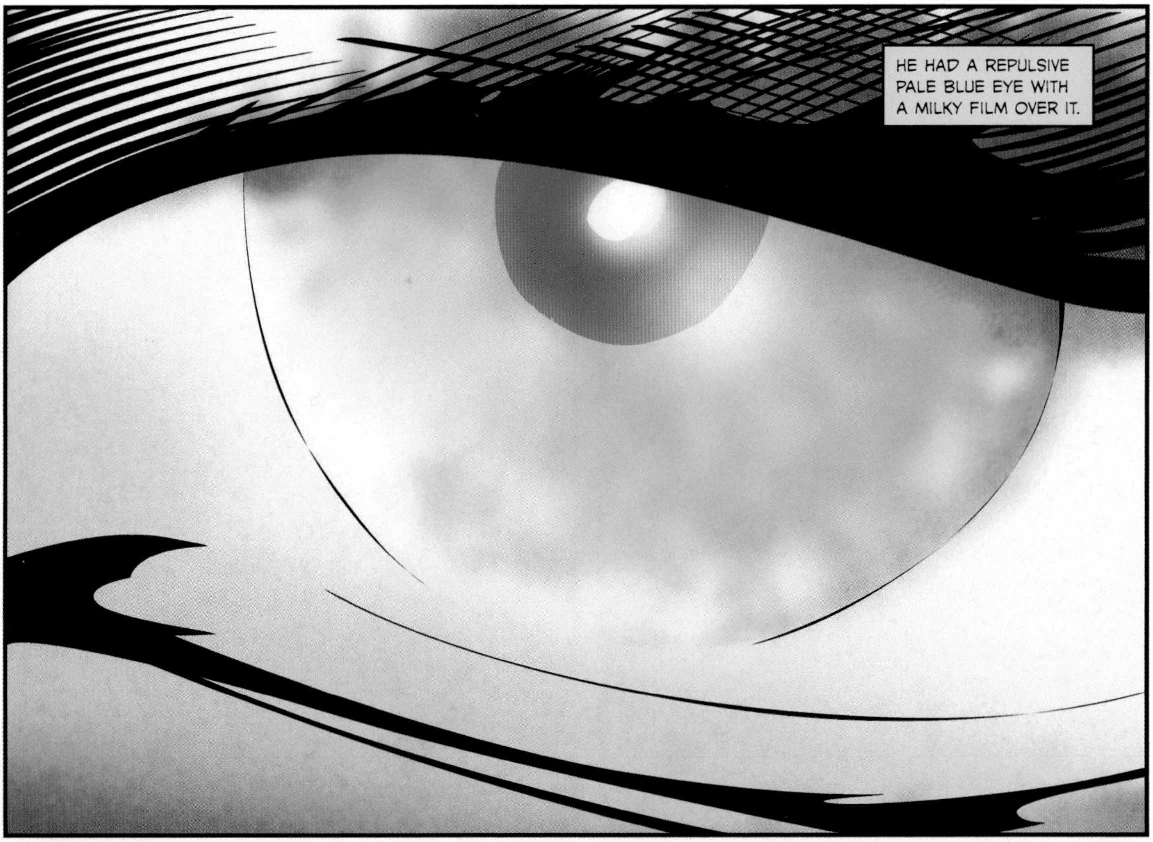
HE HAD A REPULSIVE PALE BLUE EYE WITH A MILKY FILM OVER IT.

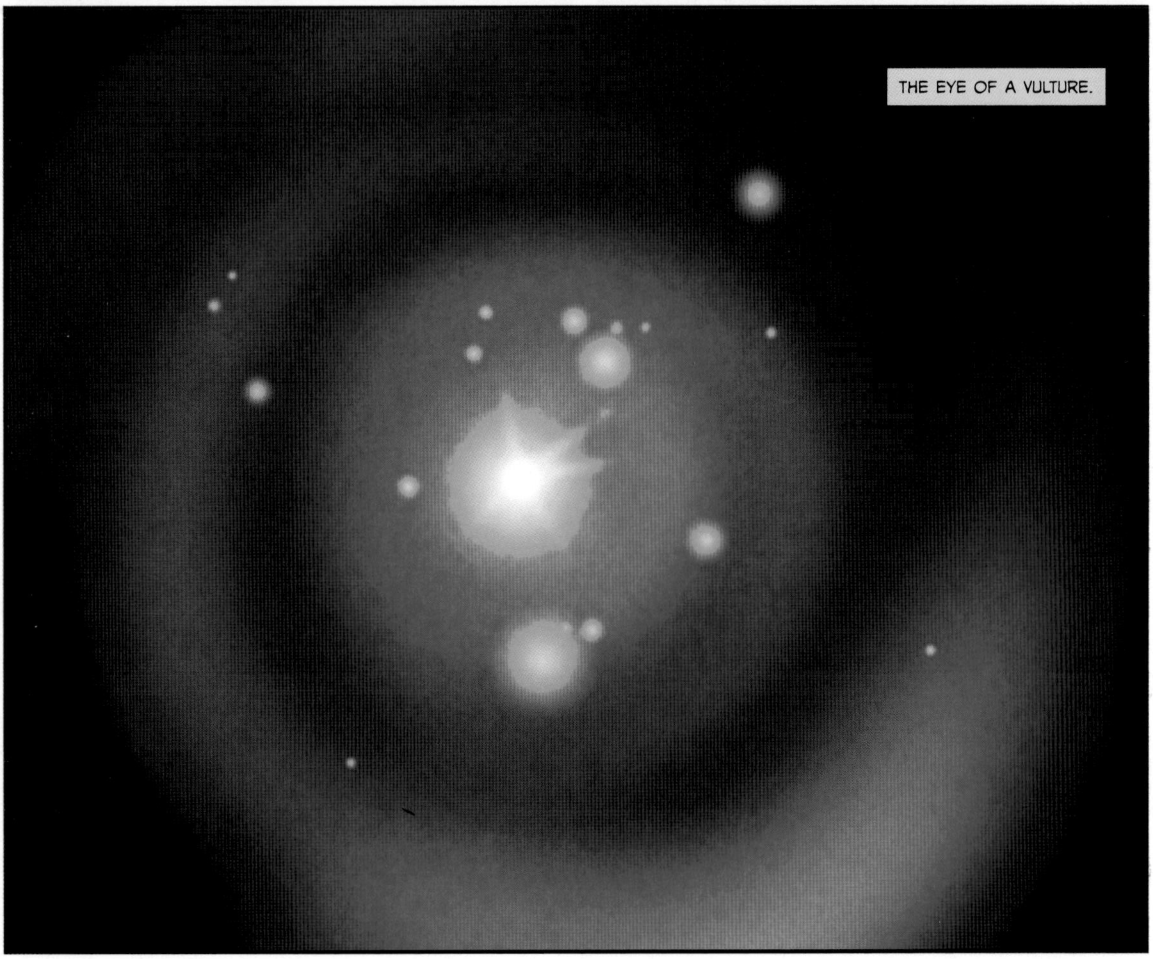
THE EYE OF A VULTURE.

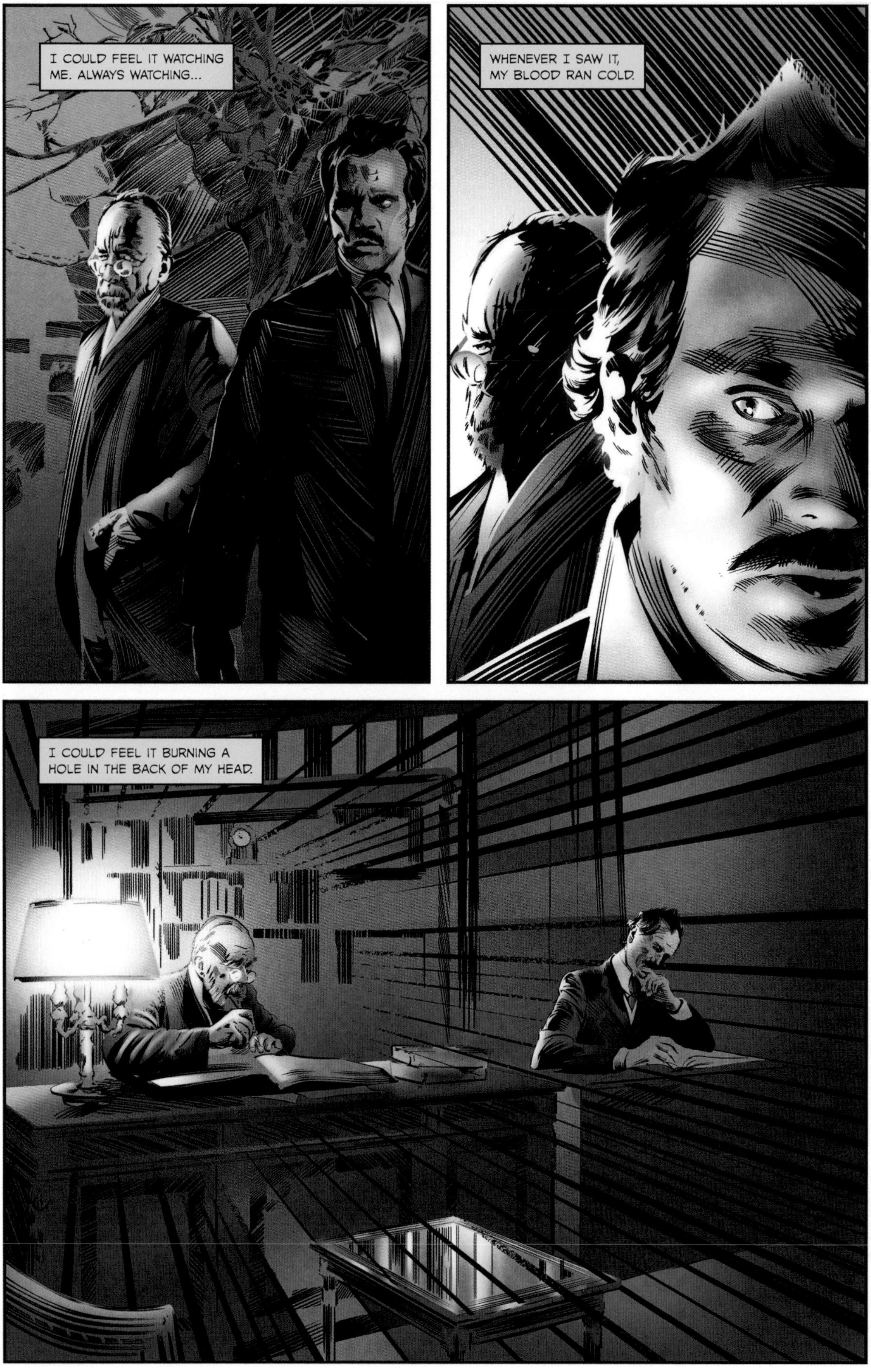
I COULD FEEL IT WATCHING ME. ALWAYS WATCHING...
WHENEVER I SAW IT, MY BLOOD RAN COLD.
I COULD FEEL IT BURNING A HOLE IN THE BACK OF MY HEAD.

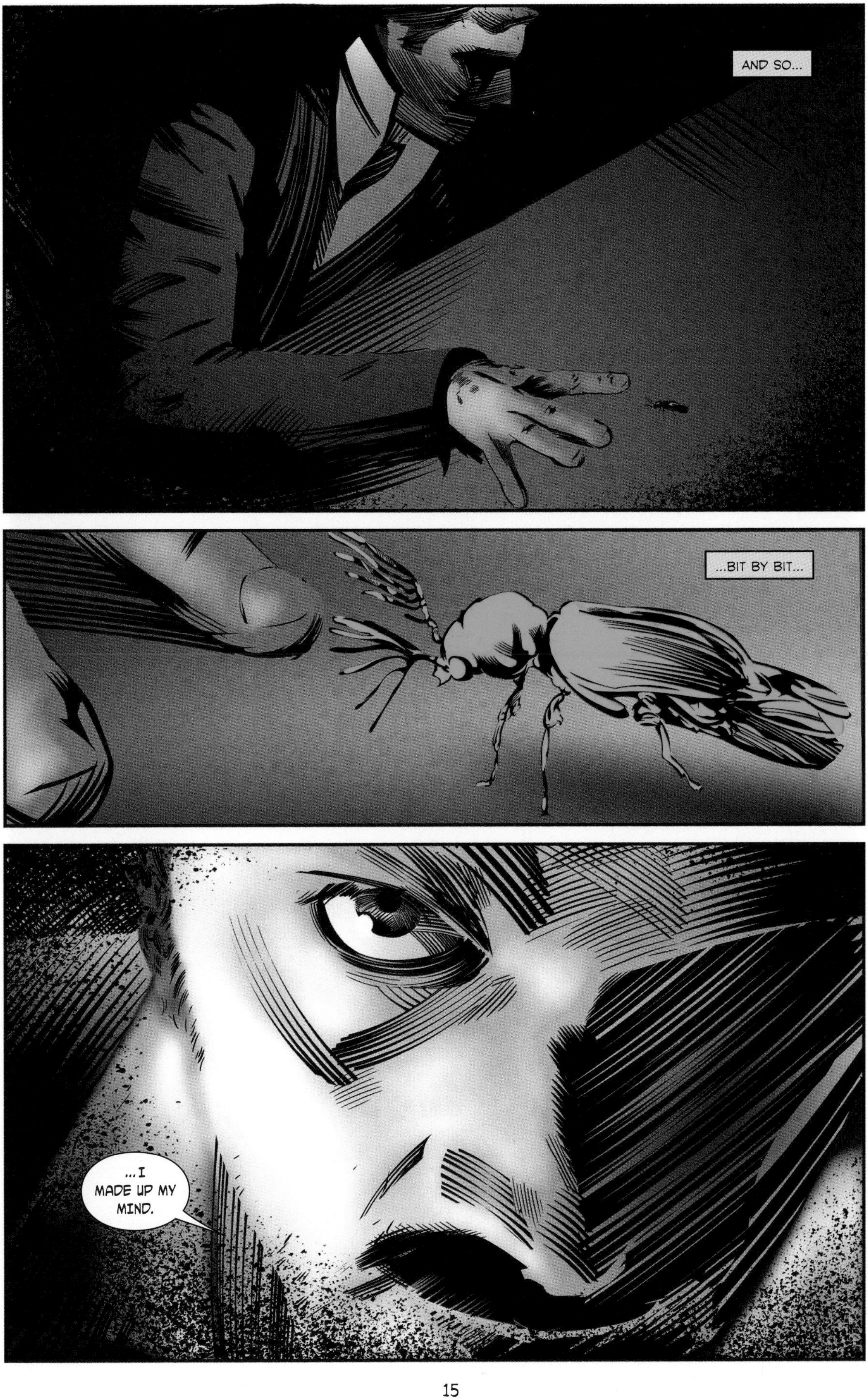

AND SO...
...BIT BY BIT...
...I MADE UP MY MIND.

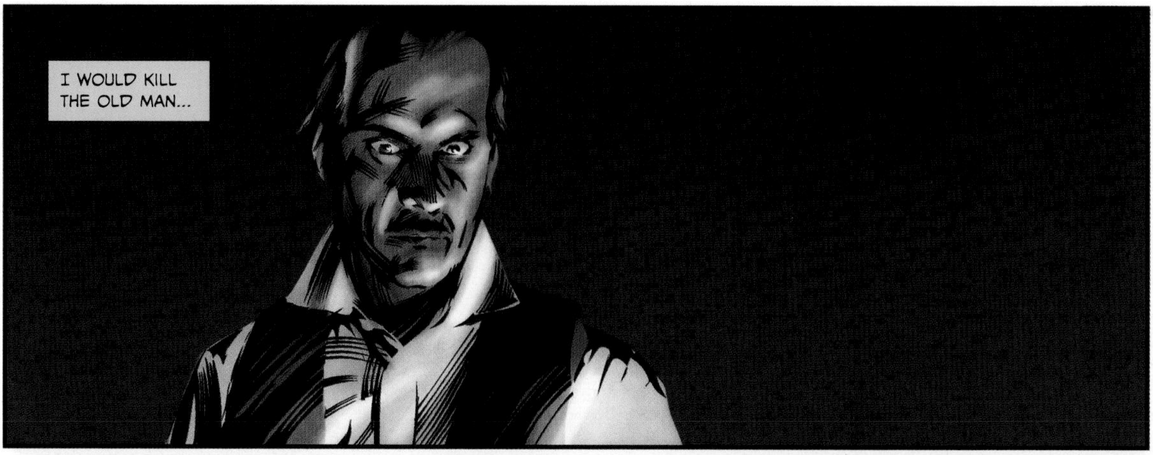
I WOULD KILL THE OLD MAN...

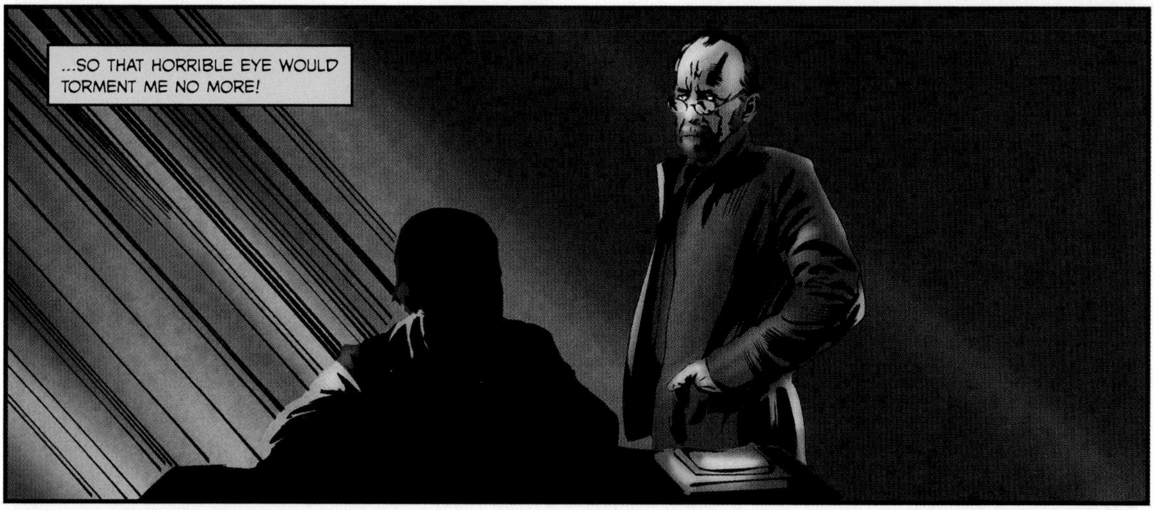
...SO THAT HORRIBLE EYE WOULD TORMENT ME NO MORE!

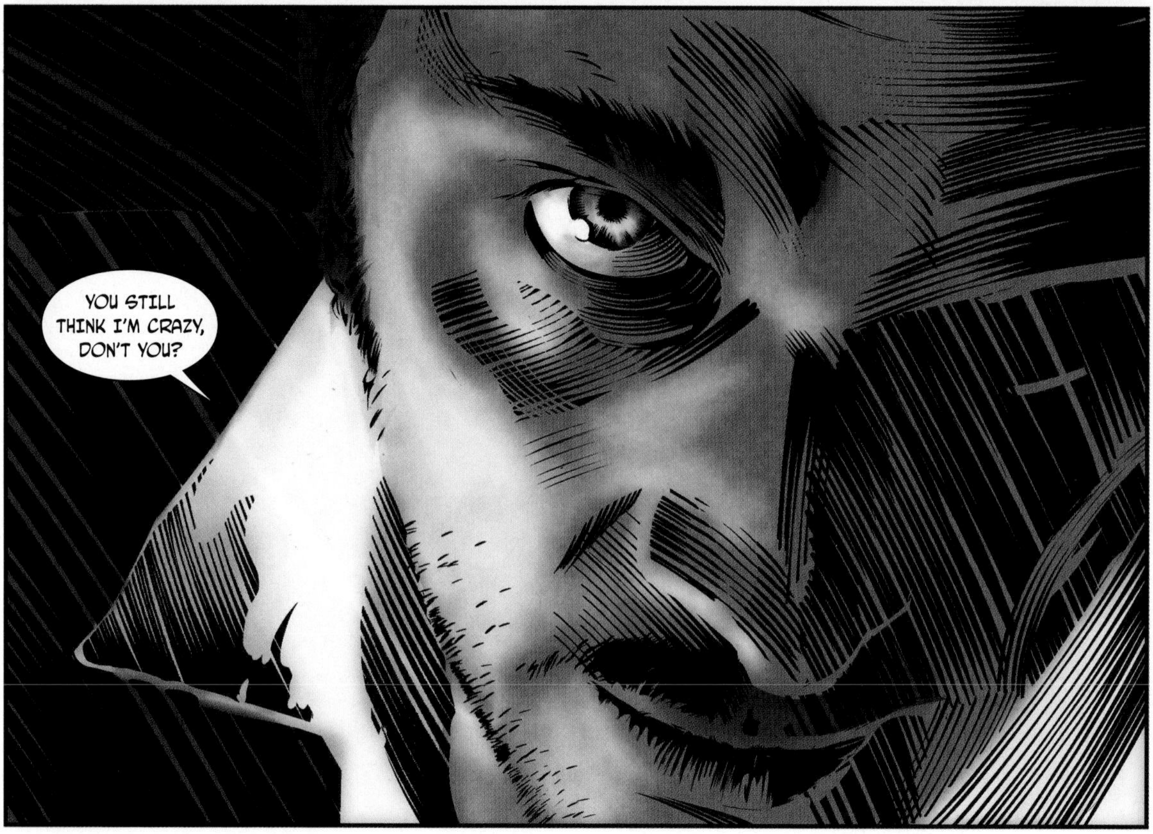
YOU STILL THINK I'M CRAZY, DON'T YOU?

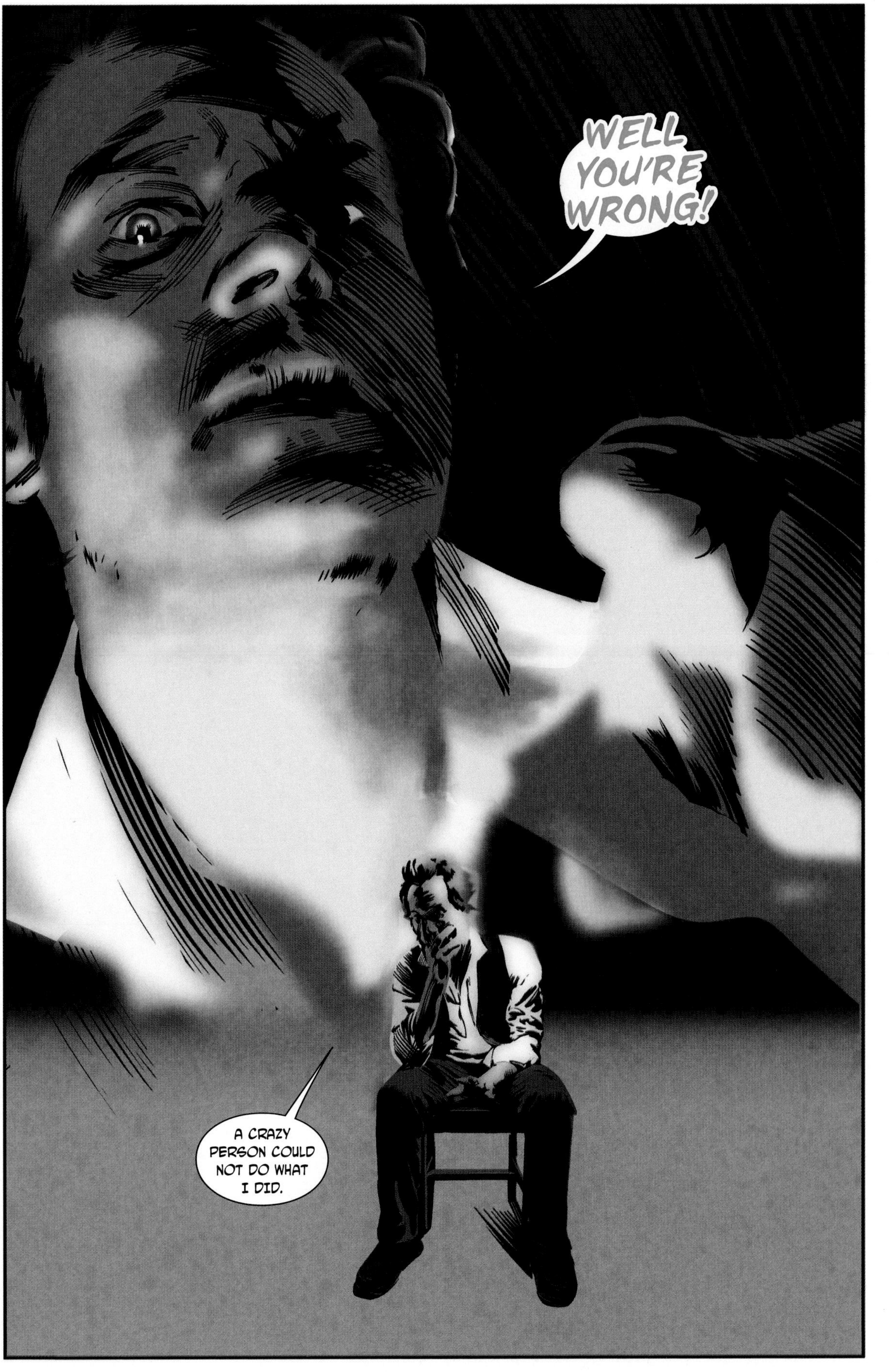
WELL YOU'RE WRONG!
A CRAZY PERSON COULD NOT DO WHAT I DID.

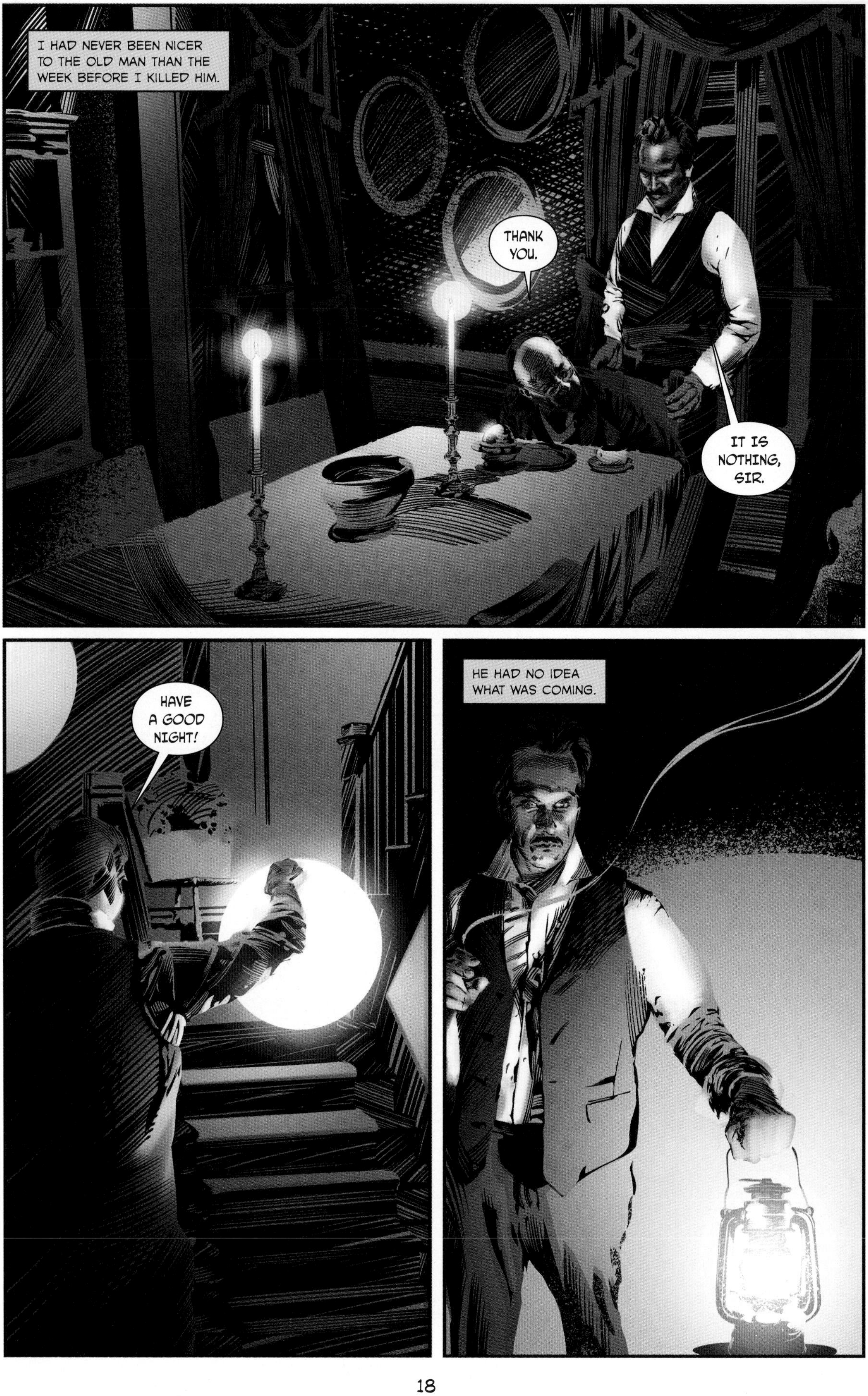
I HAD NEVER BEEN NICER TO THE OLD MAN THAN THE WEEK BEFORE I KILLED HIM.
THANK YOU.
IT IS NOTHING, SIR.
HAVE A GOOD NIGHT!
HE HAD NO IDEA WHAT WAS COMING.

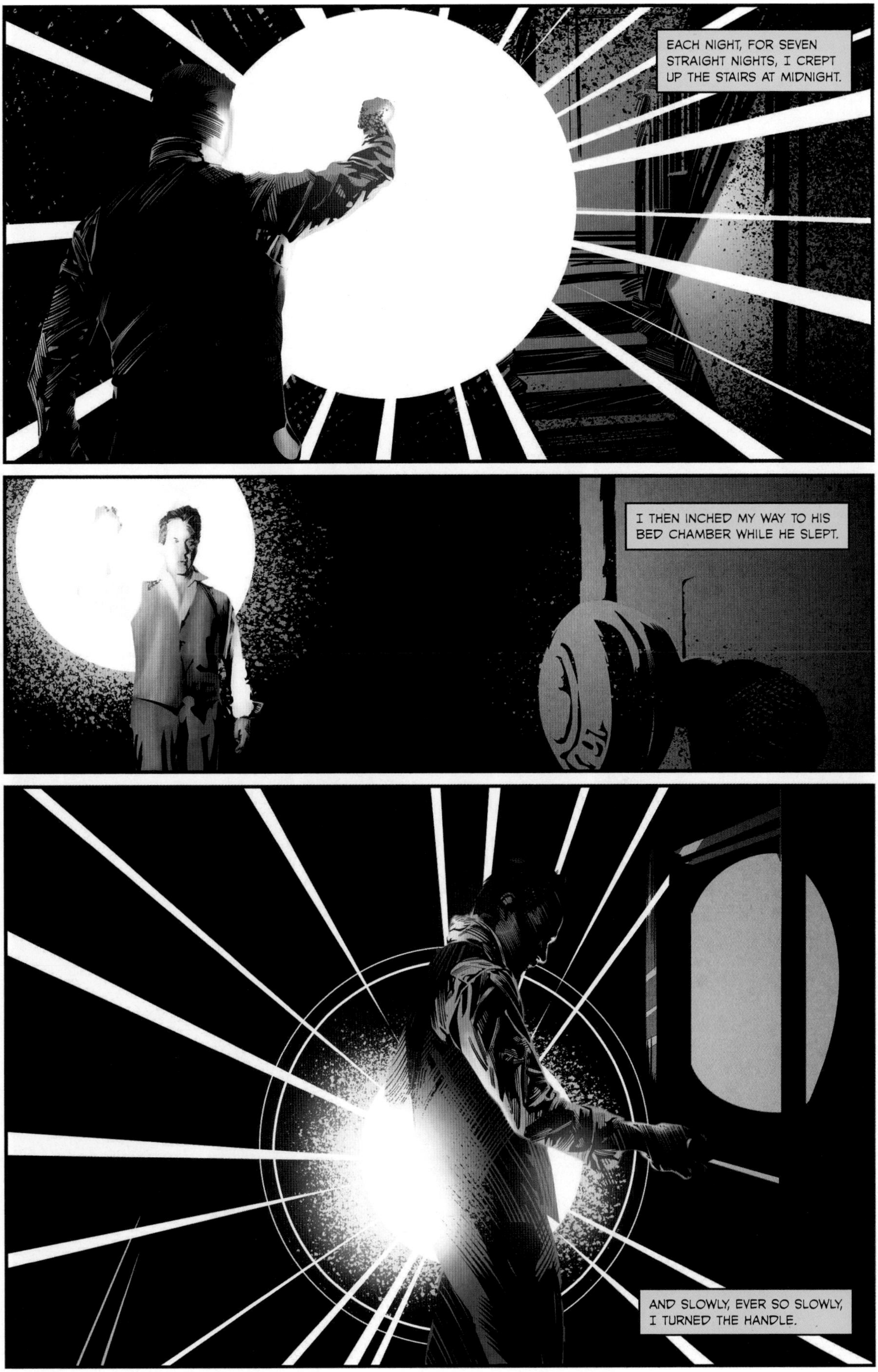
EACH NIGHT, FOR SEVEN STRAIGHT NIGHTS, I CREPT UP THE STAIRS AT MIDNIGHT.
I THEN INCHED MY WAY TO HIS BED CHAMBER WHILE HE SLEPT.
AND SLOWLY, EVER SO SLOWLY, I TURNED THE HANDLE.

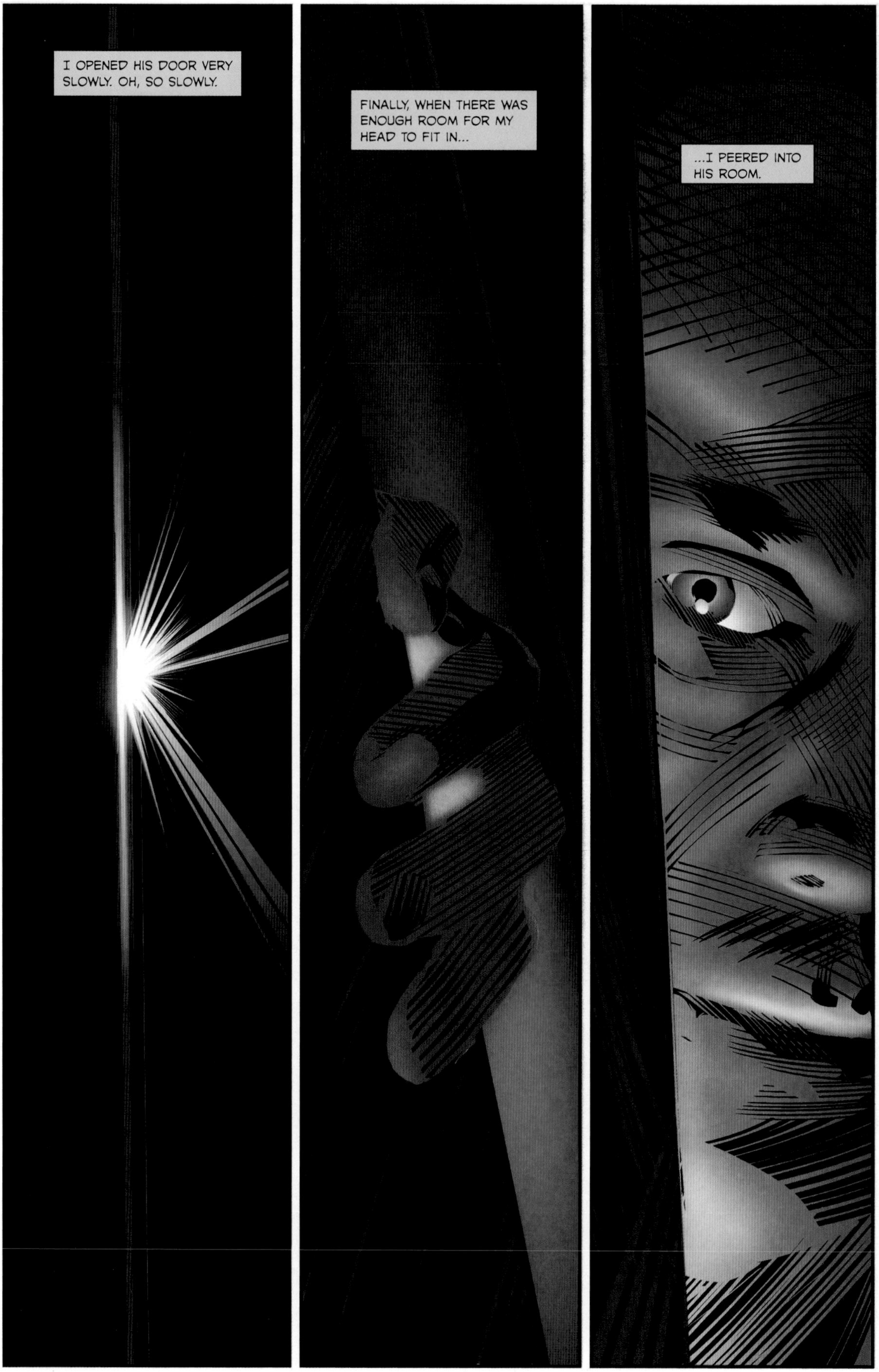
I OPENED HIS DOOR VERY SLOWLY. OH, SO SLOWLY.
FINALLY, WHEN THERE WAS ENOUGH ROOM FOR MY HEAD TO FIT IN...
...I PEERED INTO HIS ROOM.

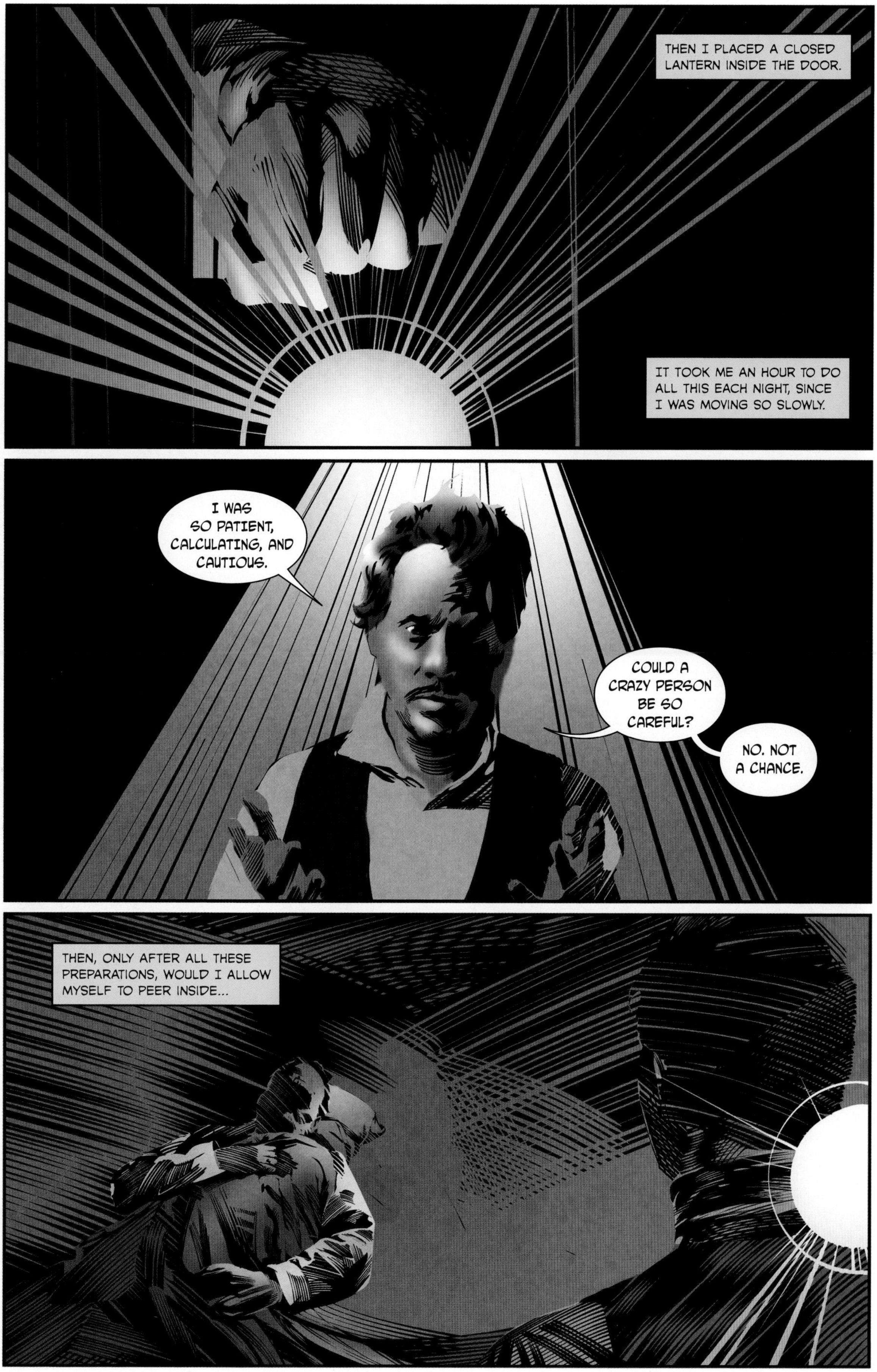
THEN I PLACED A CLOSED LANTERN INSIDE THE DOOR.
IT TOOK ME AN HOUR TO DO ALL THIS EACH NIGHT, SINCE I WAS MOVING SO SLOWLY.
I WAS SO PATIENT, CALCULATING, AND CAUTIOUS.
COULD A CRAZY PERSON BE SO CAREFUL?
NO. NOT A CHANCE.
THEN, ONLY AFTER ALL THESE PREPARATIONS, WOULD I ALLOW MYSELF TO PEER INSIDE...

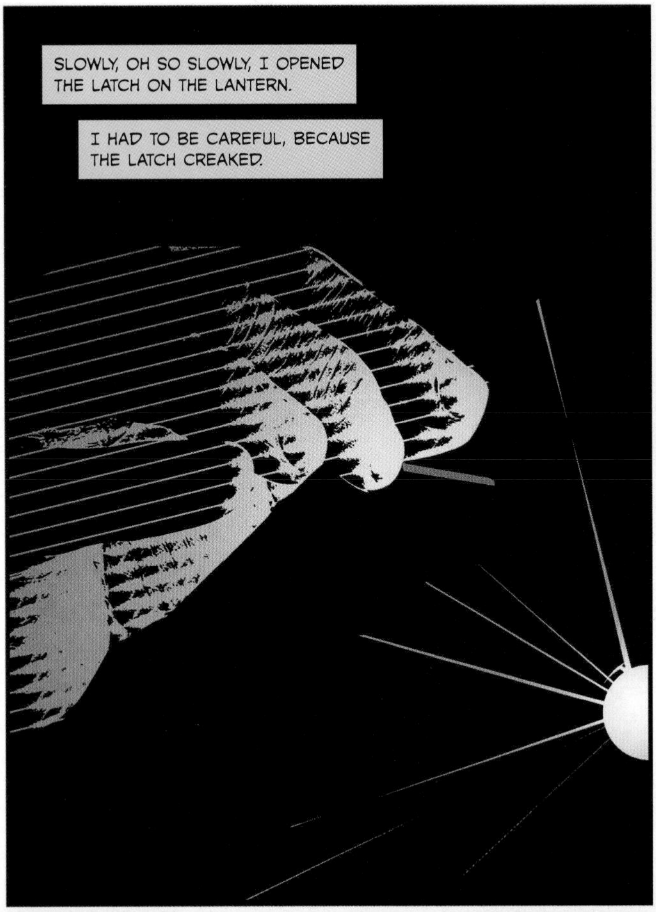
SLOWLY, OH SO SLOWLY, I OPENED THE LATCH ON THE LANTERN.
I HAD TO BE CAREFUL, BECAUSE THE LATCH CREAKED.

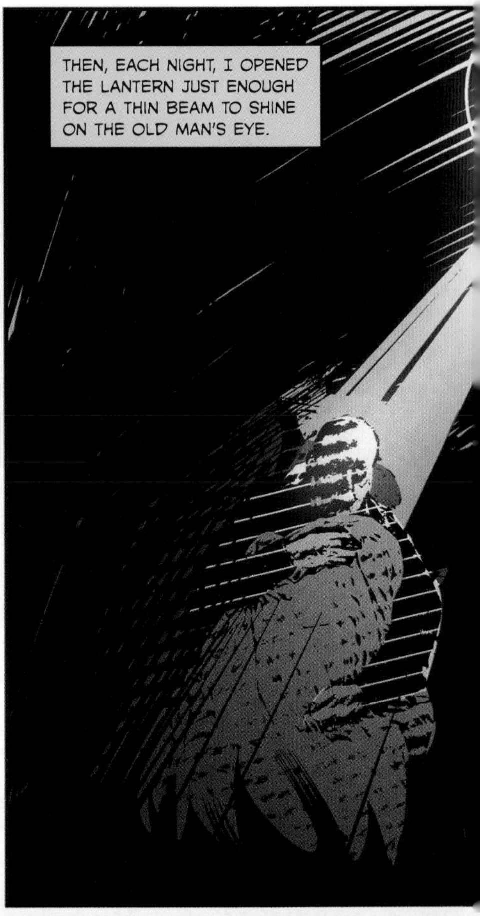
THEN, EACH NIGHT, I OPENED THE LANTERN JUST ENOUGH FOR A THIN BEAM TO SHINE ON THE OLD MAN'S EYE.

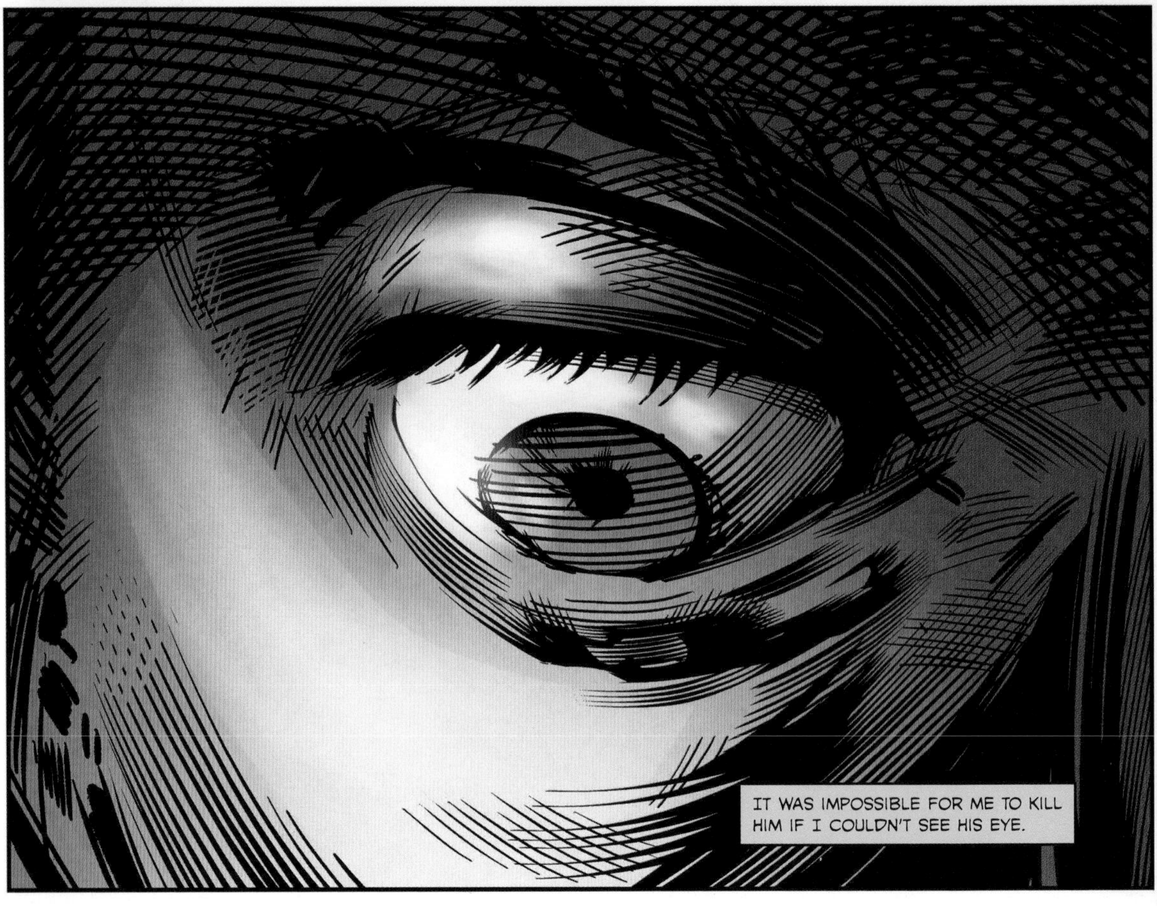
IT WAS IMPOSSIBLE FOR ME TO KILL HIM IF I COULDN'T SEE HIS EYE.

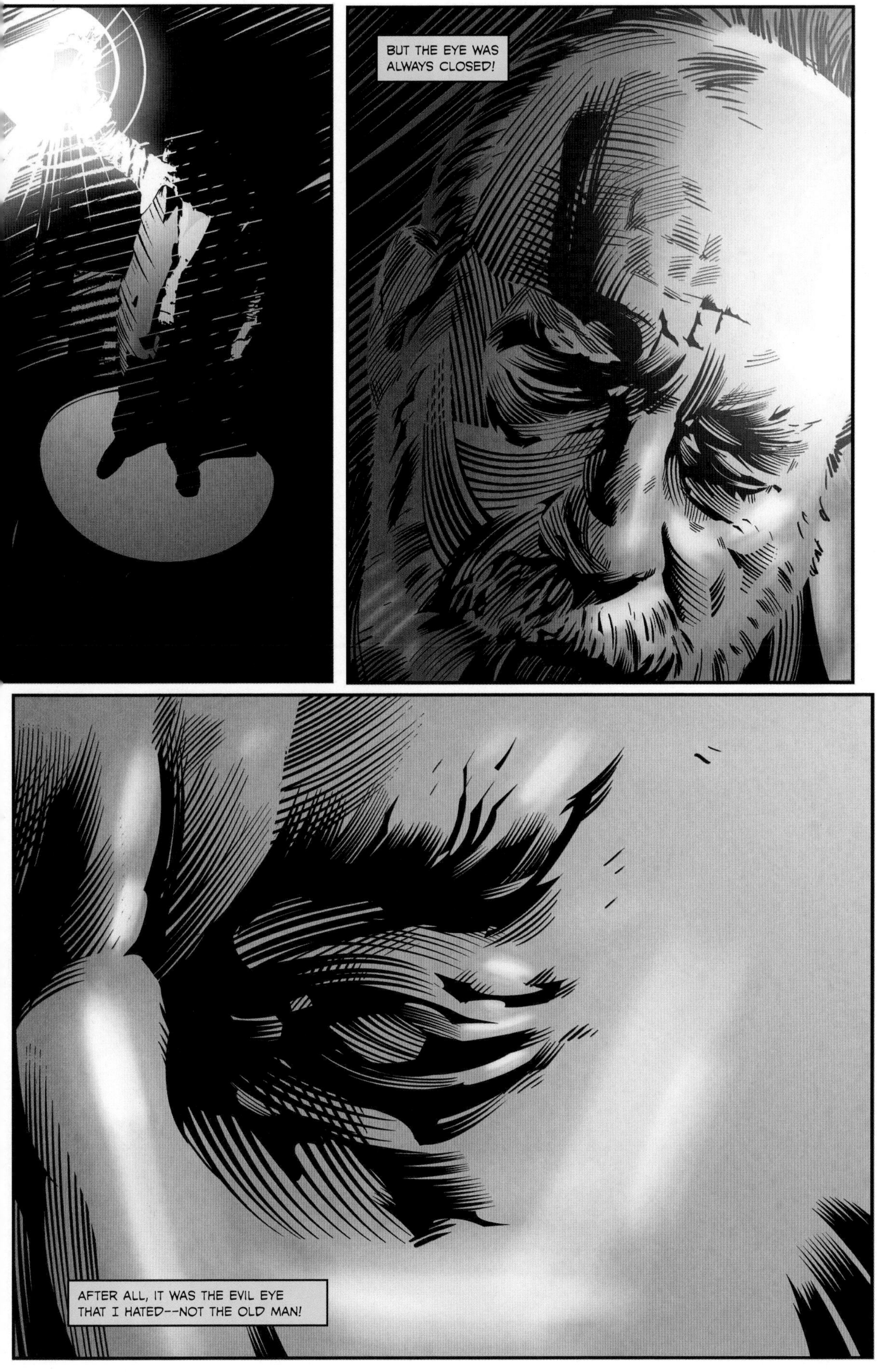
BUT THE EYE WAS ALWAYS CLOSED!
AFTER ALL, IT WAS THE EVIL EYE THAT I HATED--NOT THE OLD MAN!

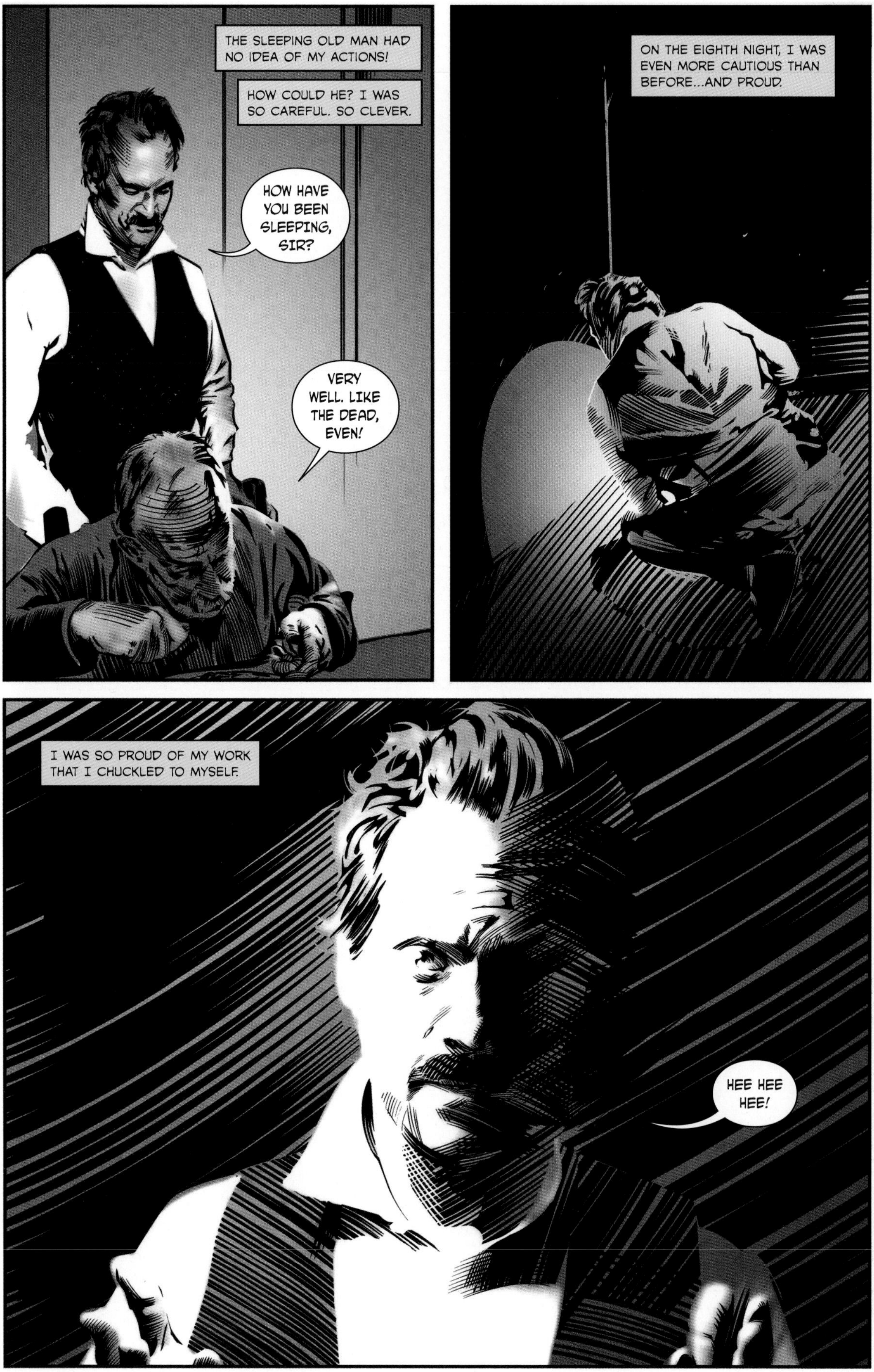
THE SLEEPING OLD MAN HAD NO IDEA OF MY ACTIONS!
HOW COULD HE? I WAS SO CAREFUL. SO CLEVER.
HOW HAVE YOU BEEN SLEEPING, SIR?
VERY WELL. LIKE THE DEAD, EVEN!
ON THE EIGHTH NIGHT, I WAS EVEN MORE CAUTIOUS THAN BEFORE...AND PROUD.
I WAS SO PROUD OF MY WORK THAT I CHUCKLED TO MYSELF.
HEE HEE HEE!

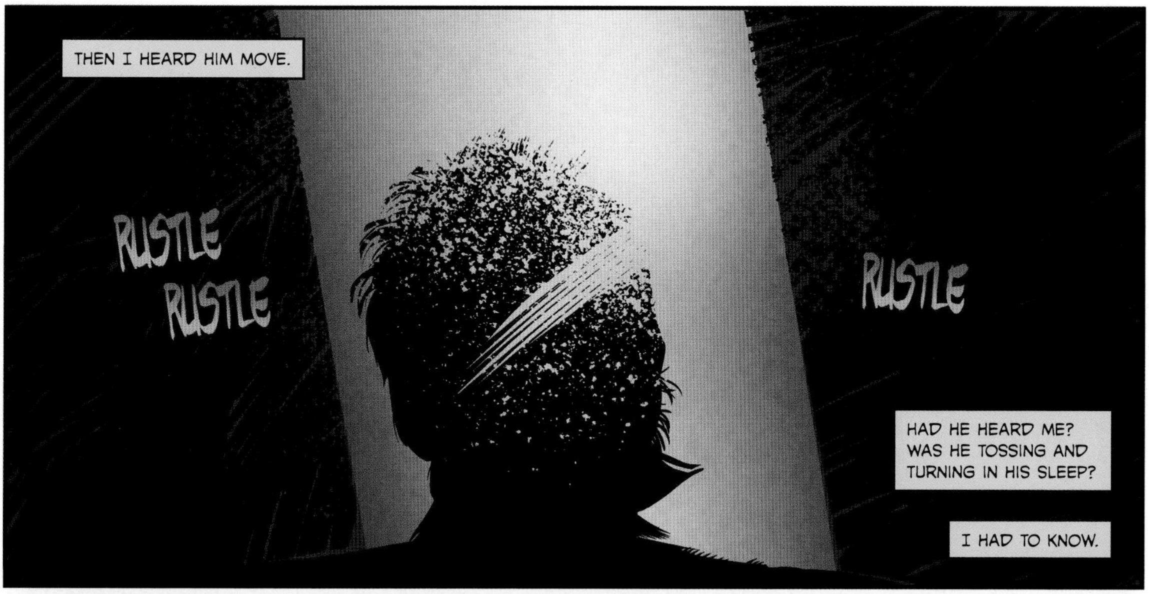
THEN I HEARD HIM MOVE.
RUSTLE
RUSTLE
RUSTLE
HAD HE HEARD ME? WAS HE TOSSING AND TURNING IN HIS SLEEP?
I HAD TO KNOW.

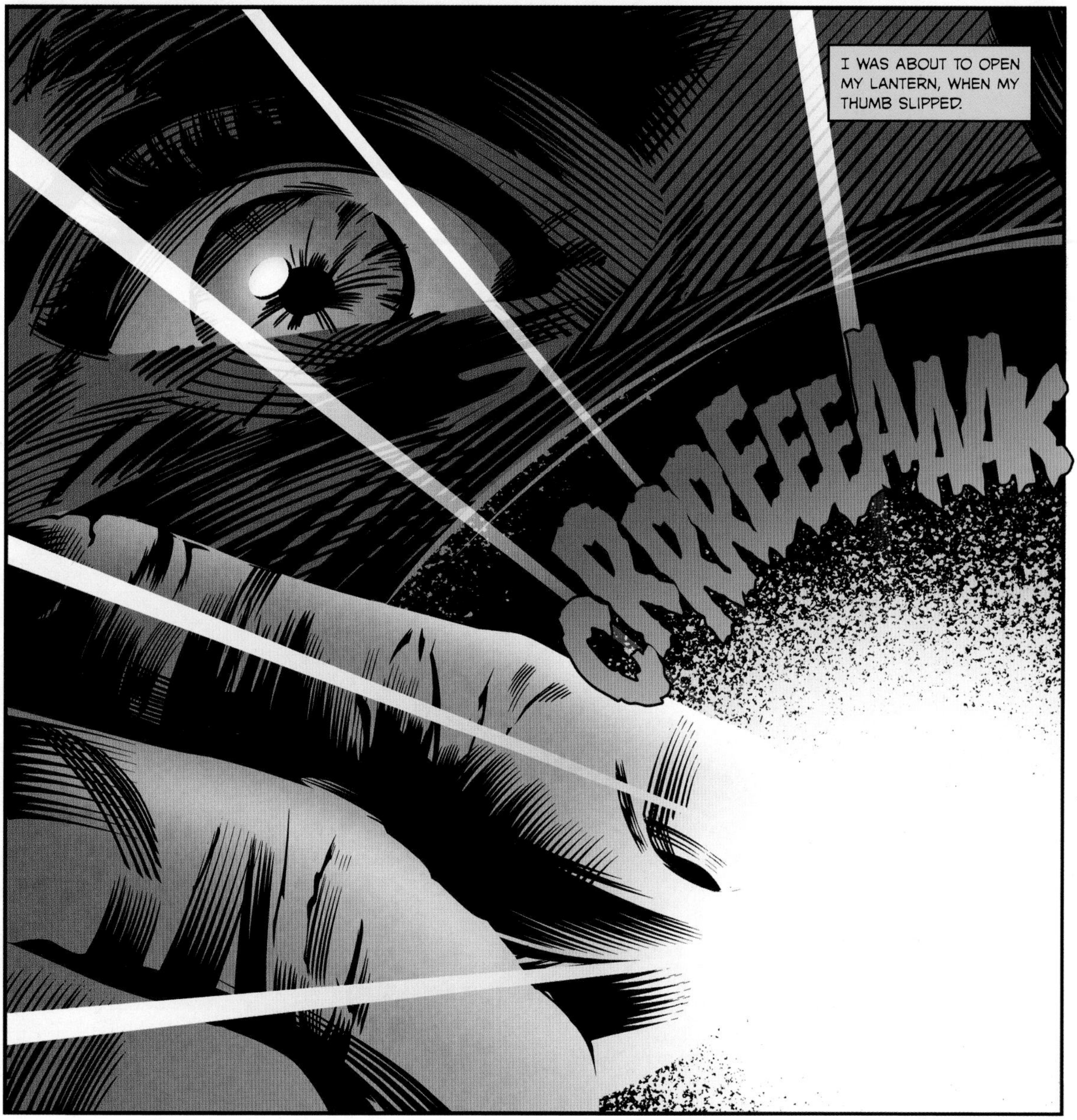
I WAS ABOUT TO OPEN MY LANTERN, WHEN MY THUMB SLIPPED.
CRREEEAAAK

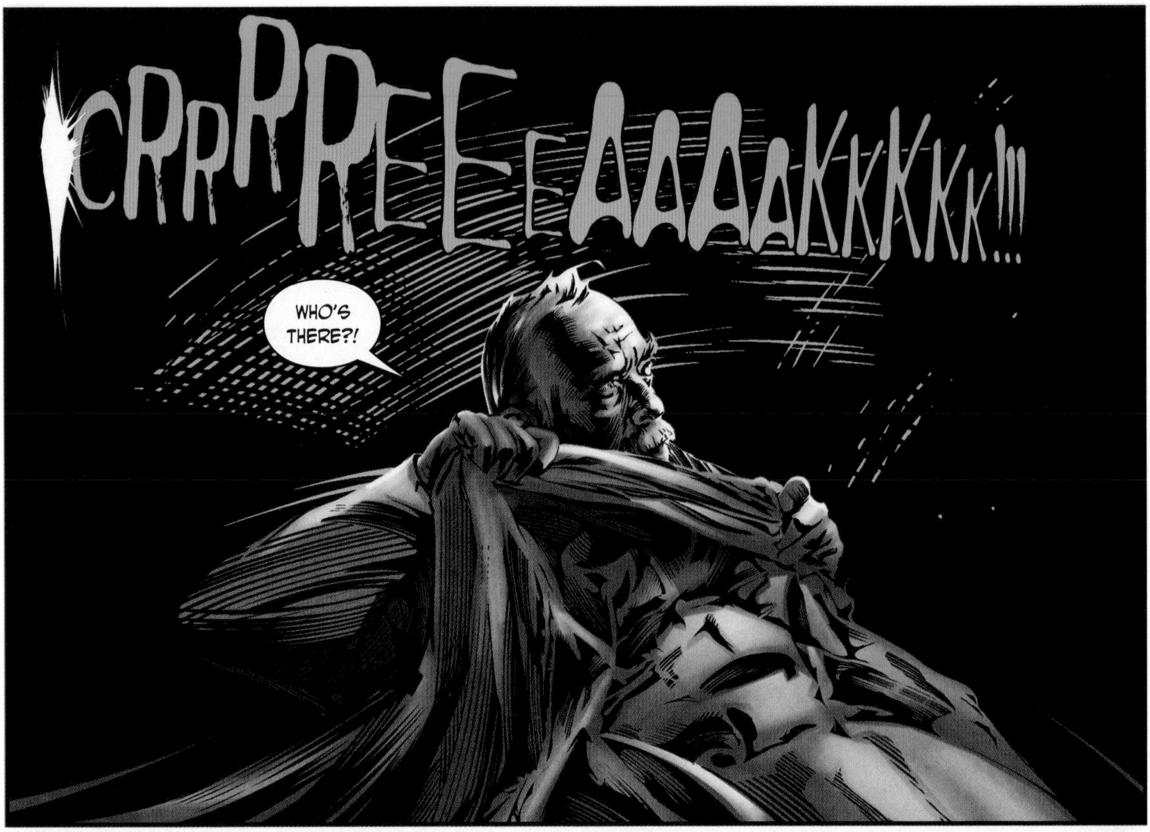
CRRRRREEEEAAAAKKKKK!!!
WHO'S THERE?!

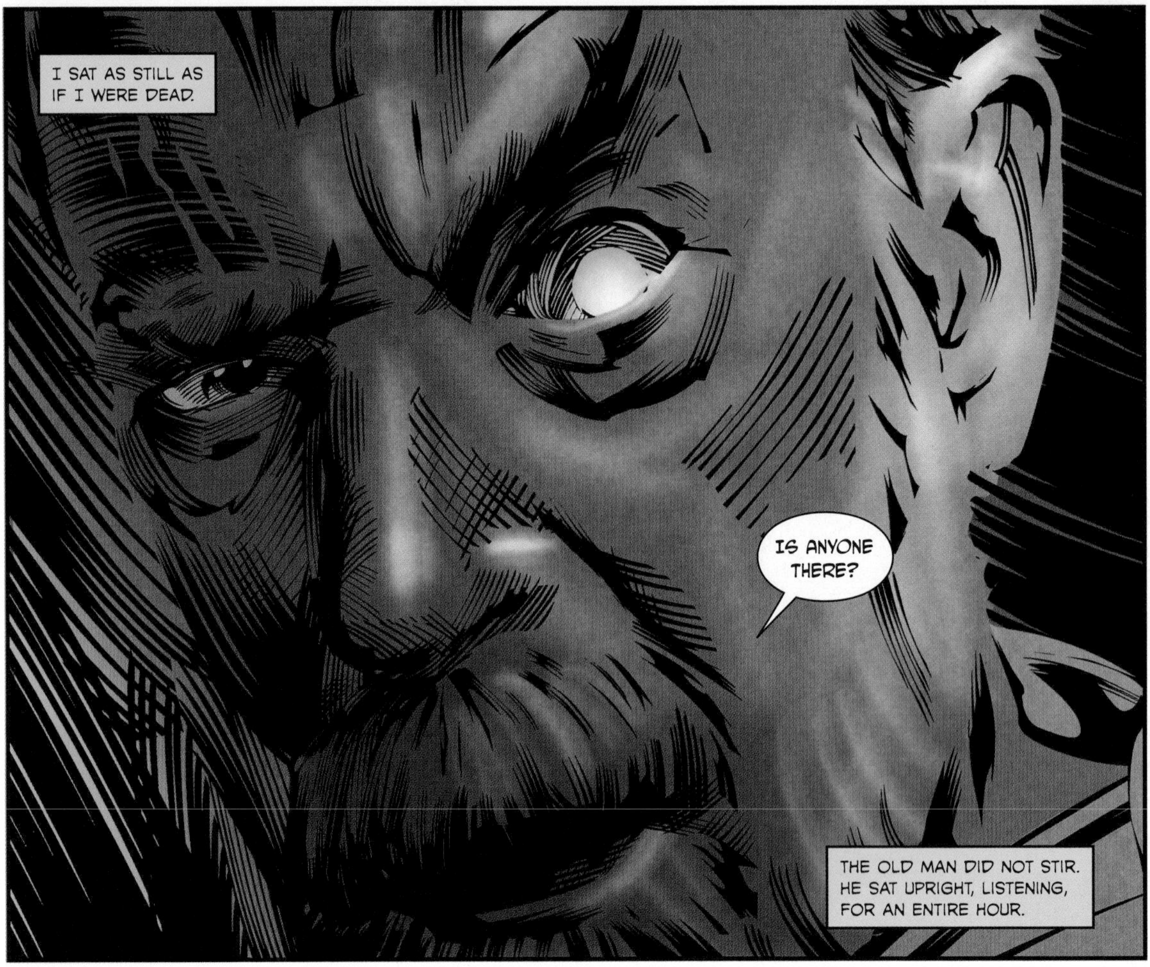
I SAT AS STILL AS IF I WERE DEAD.
IS ANYONE THERE?
THE OLD MAN DID NOT STIR. HE SAT UPRIGHT, LISTENING, FOR AN ENTIRE HOUR.

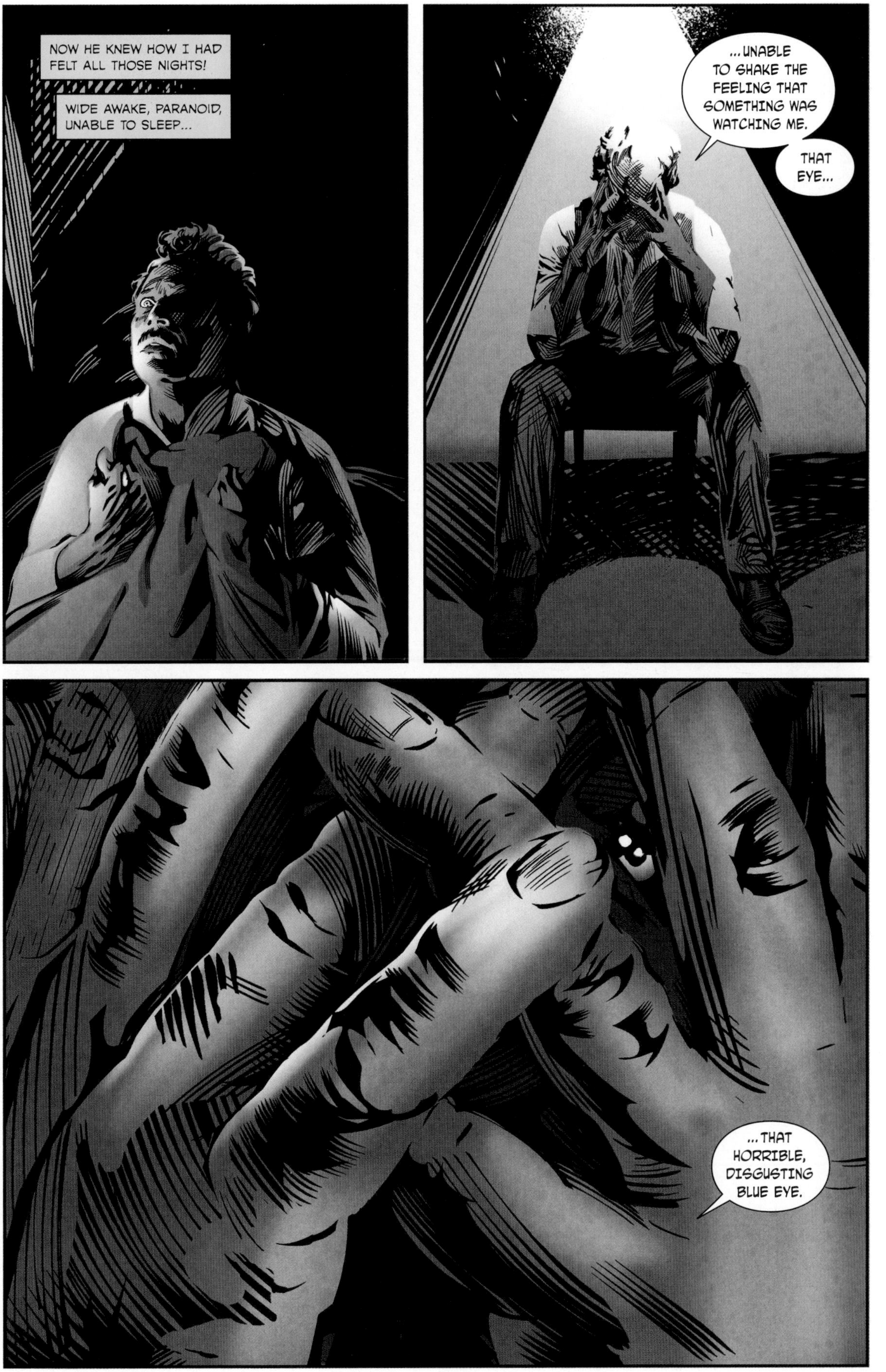
NOW HE KNEW HOW I HAD FELT ALL THOSE NIGHTS!
WIDE AWAKE, PARANOID, UNABLE TO SLEEP...
...UNABLE TO SHAKE THE FEELING THAT SOMETHING WAS WATCHING ME.
THAT EYE...
...THAT HORRIBLE, DISGUSTING BLUE EYE.

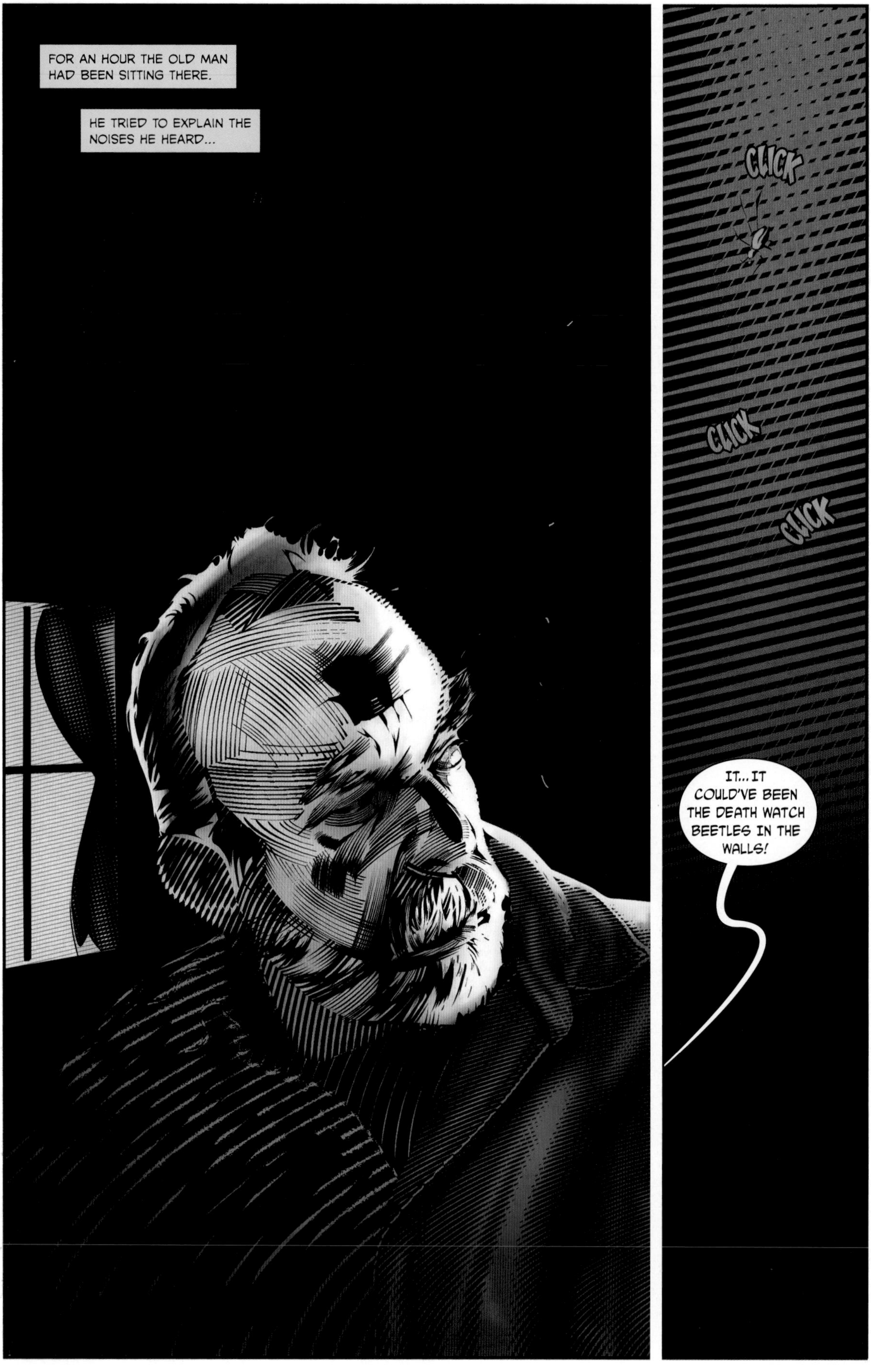

FOR AN HOUR THE OLD MAN HAD BEEN SITTING THERE.
HE TRIED TO EXPLAIN THE NOISES HE HEARD...
CLICK
CLICK
CLICK
IT... IT COULD'VE BEEN THE DEATH WATCH BEETLES IN THE WALLS!

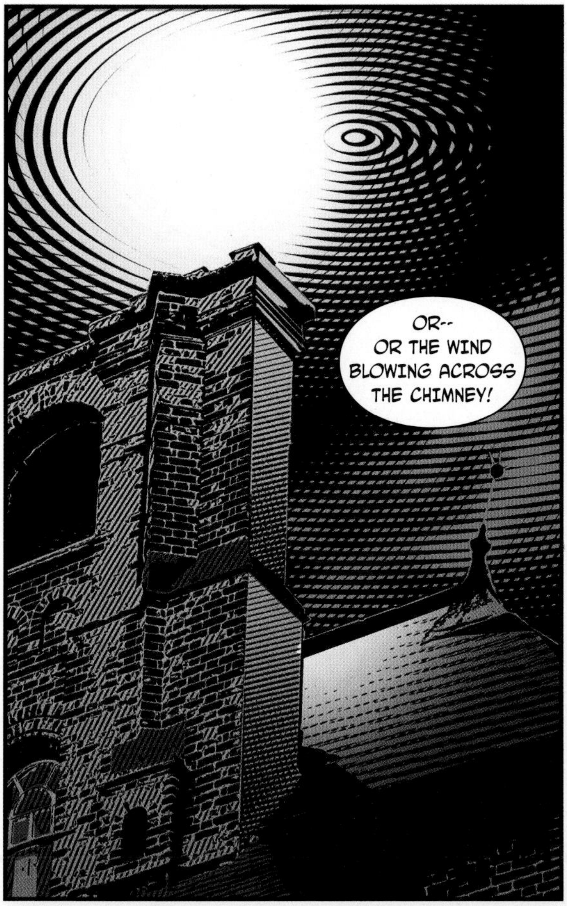
OR--
OR THE WIND BLOWING ACROSS THE CHIMNEY!

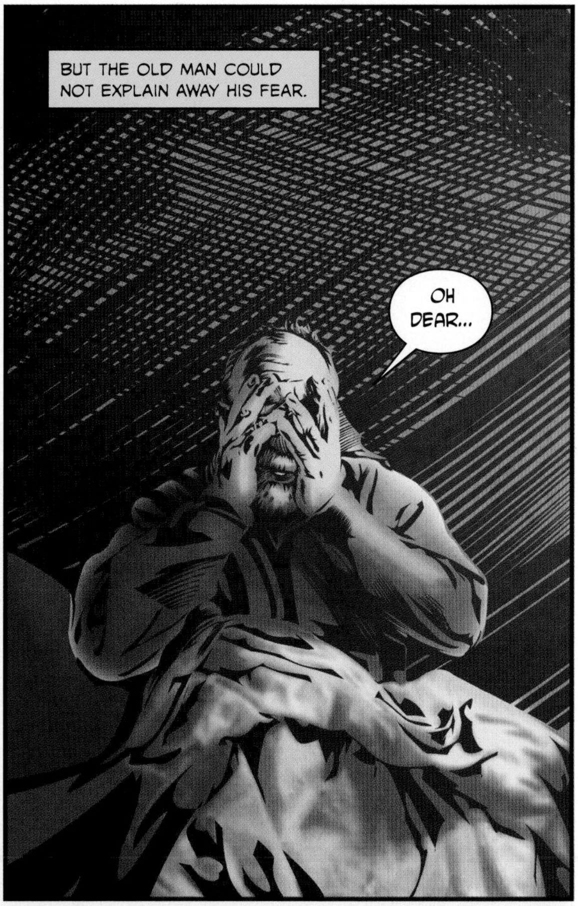
BUT THE OLD MAN COULD NOT EXPLAIN AWAY HIS FEAR.
OH DEAR...

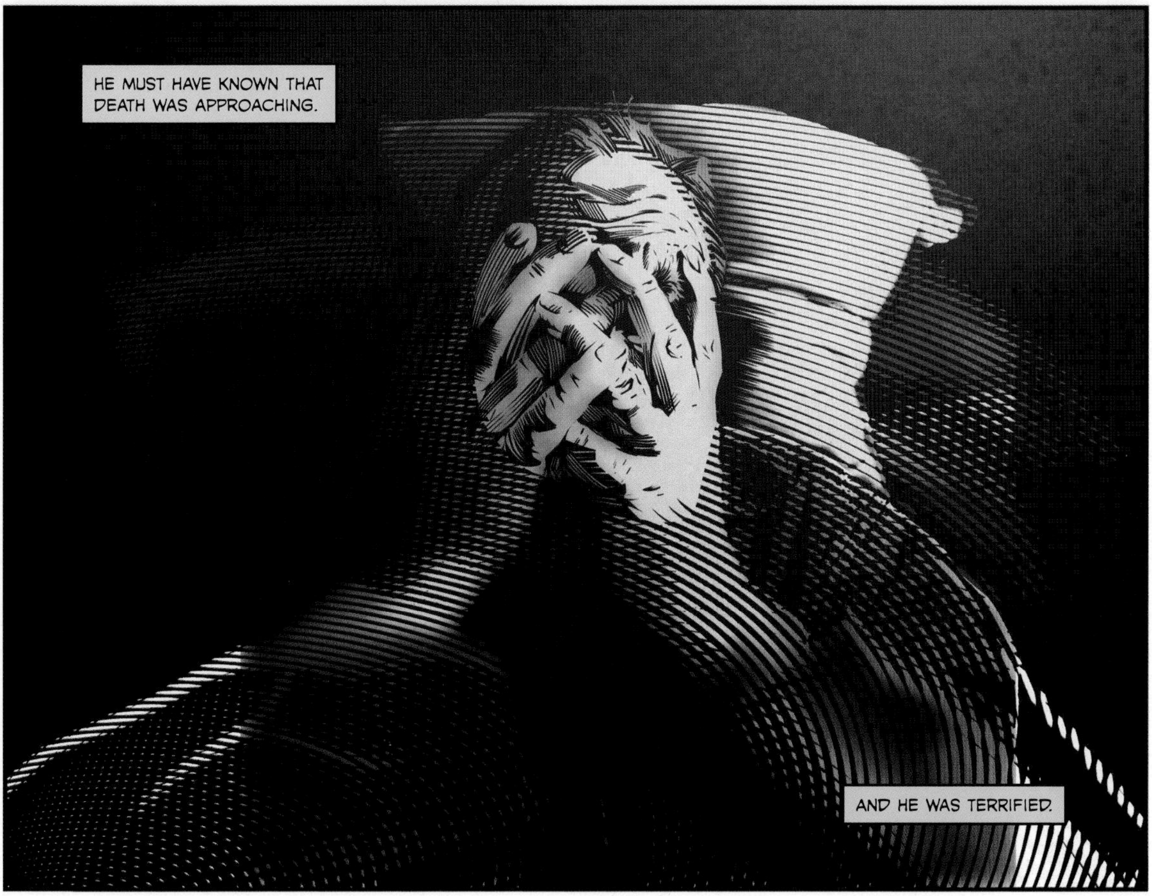
HE MUST HAVE KNOWN THAT DEATH WAS APPROACHING.
AND HE WAS TERRIFIED.

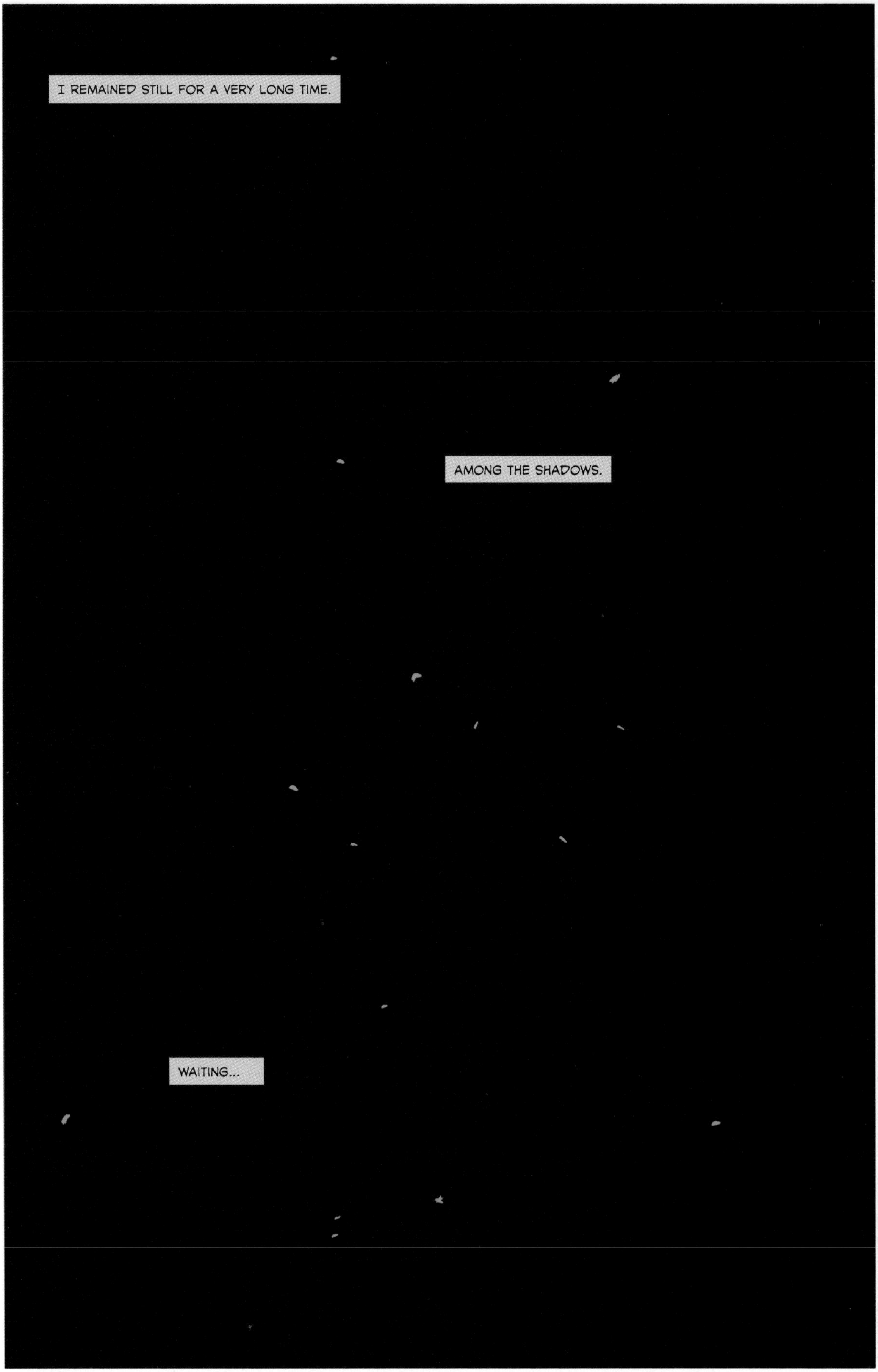
I REMAINED STILL FOR A VERY LONG TIME.
AMONG THE SHADOWS.
WAITING...

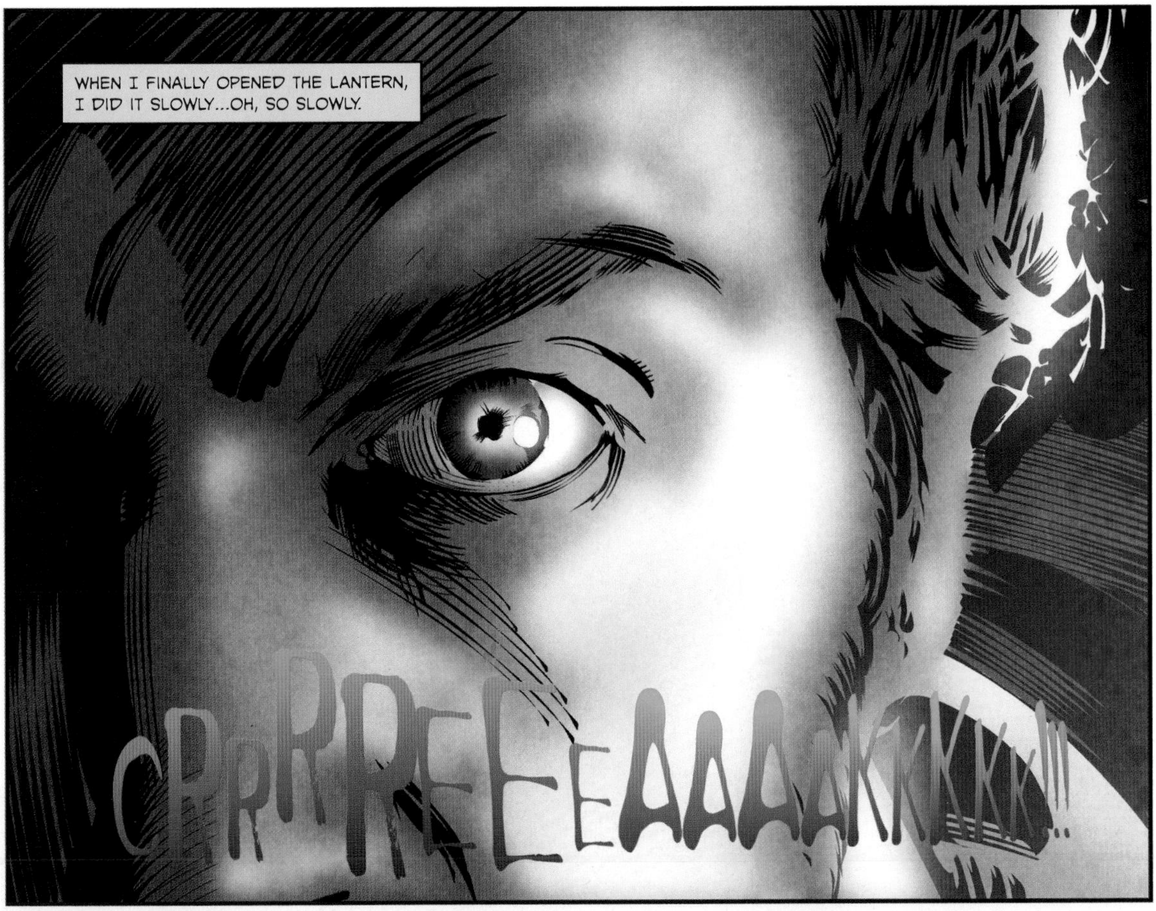
WHEN I FINALLY OPENED THE LANTERN, I DID IT SLOWLY...OH, SO SLOWLY.
CRRRREEEAAAAKKKKK!!!

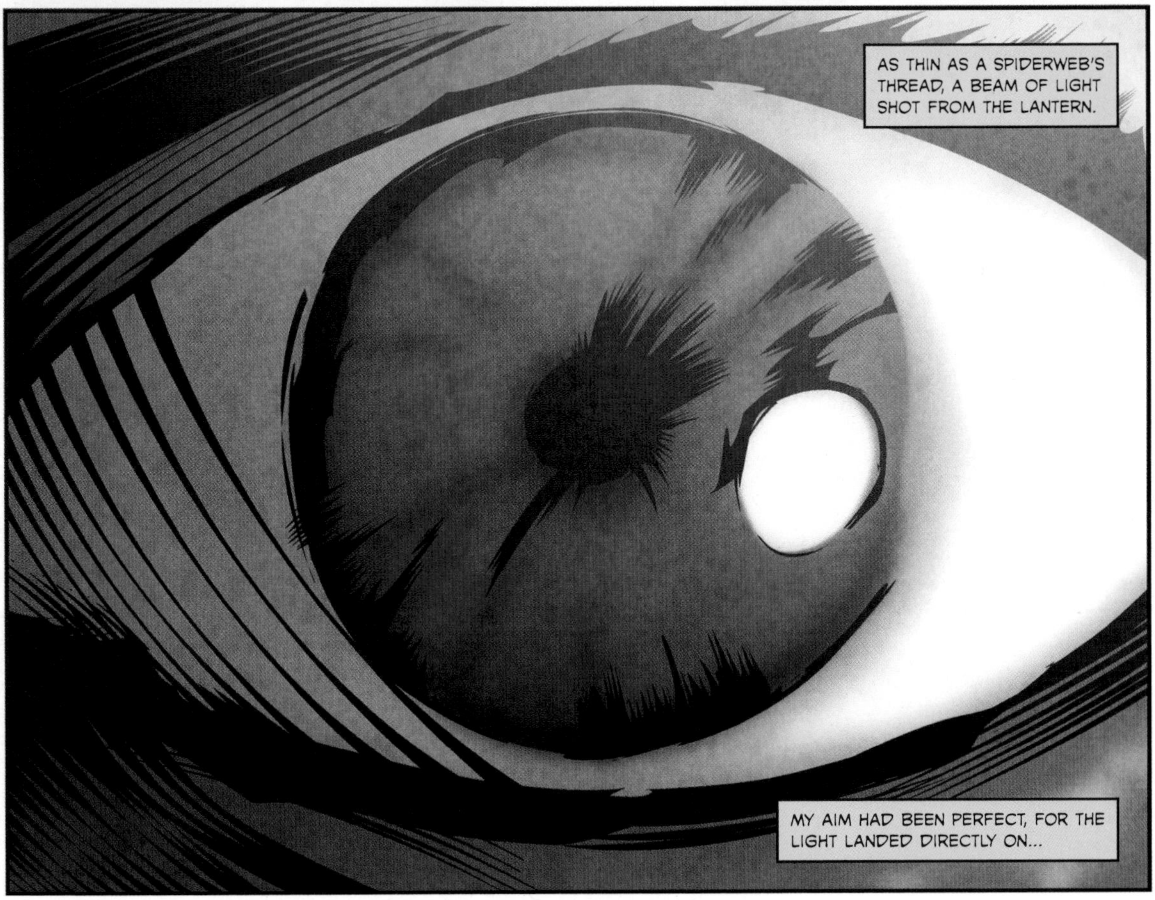
AS THIN AS A SPIDERWEB'S THREAD, A BEAM OF LIGHT SHOT FROM THE LANTERN.
MY AIM HAD BEEN PERFECT, FOR THE LIGHT LANDED DIRECTLY ON...

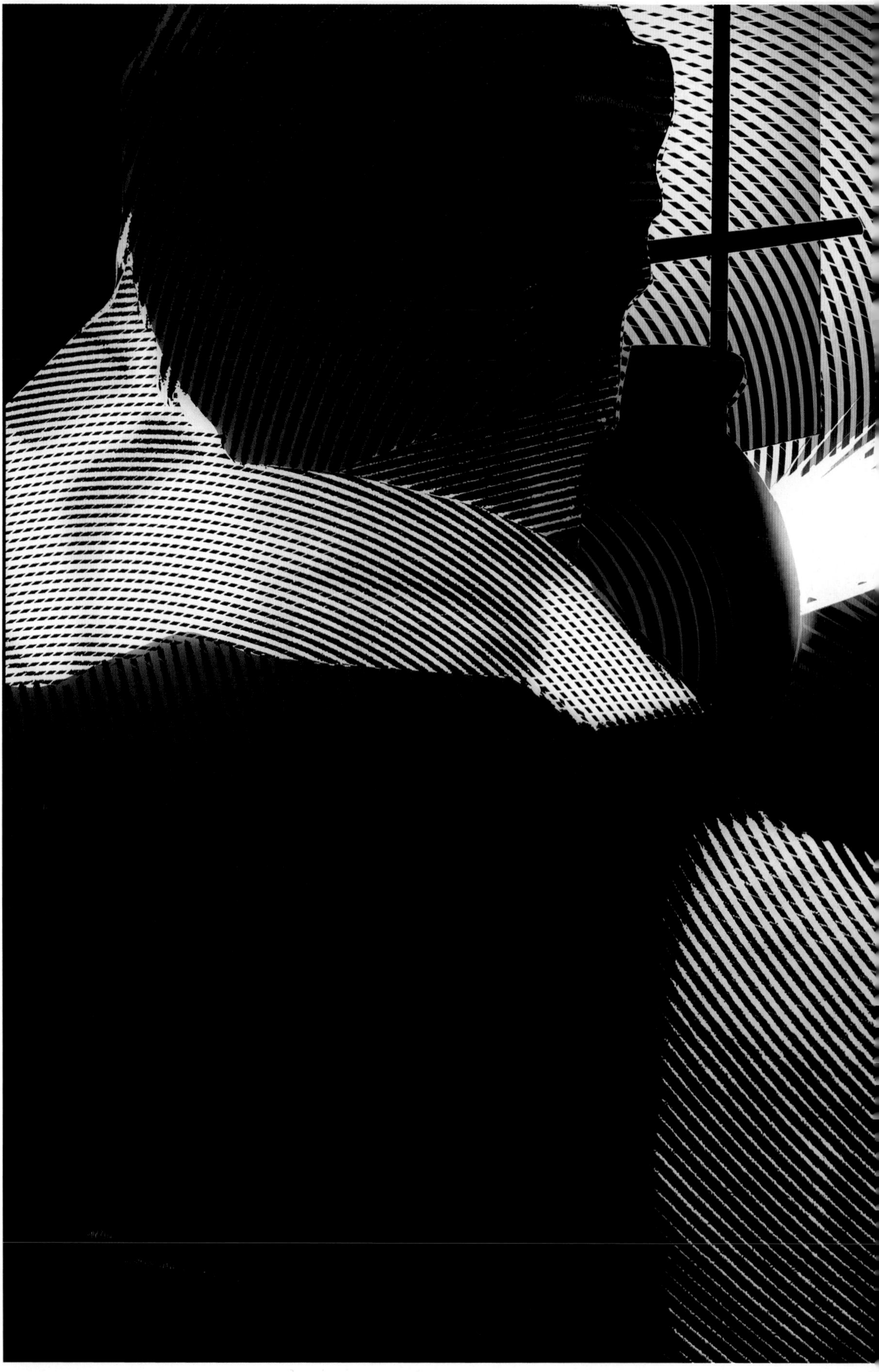

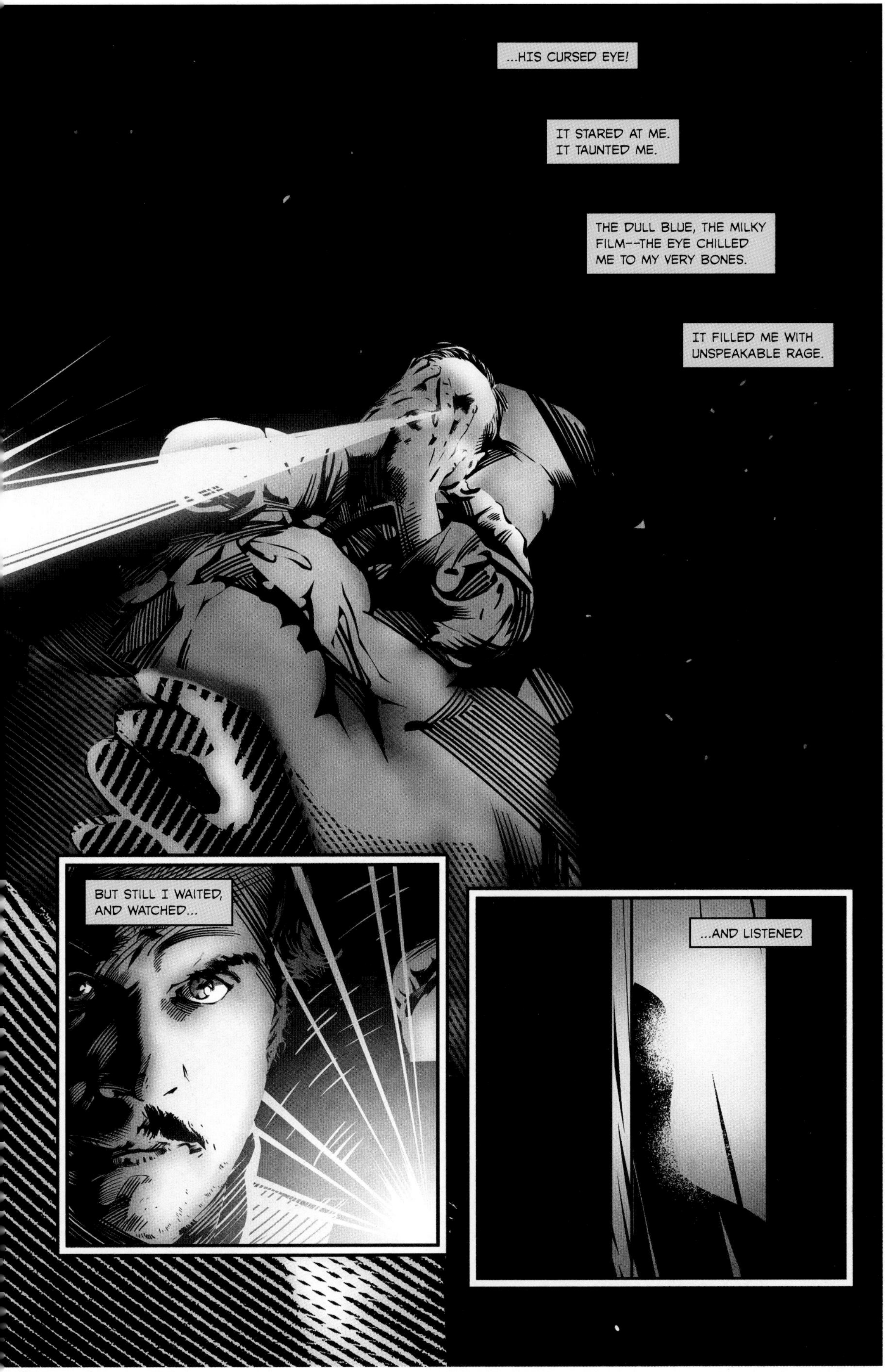
...HIS CURSED EYE!
IT STARED AT ME.
IT TAUNTED ME.
THE DULL BLUE, THE MILKY
FILM--THE EYE CHILLED
ME TO MY VERY BONES.
IT FILLED ME WITH
UNSPEAKABLE RAGE.
BUT STILL I WAITED,
AND WATCHED...
...AND LISTENED.

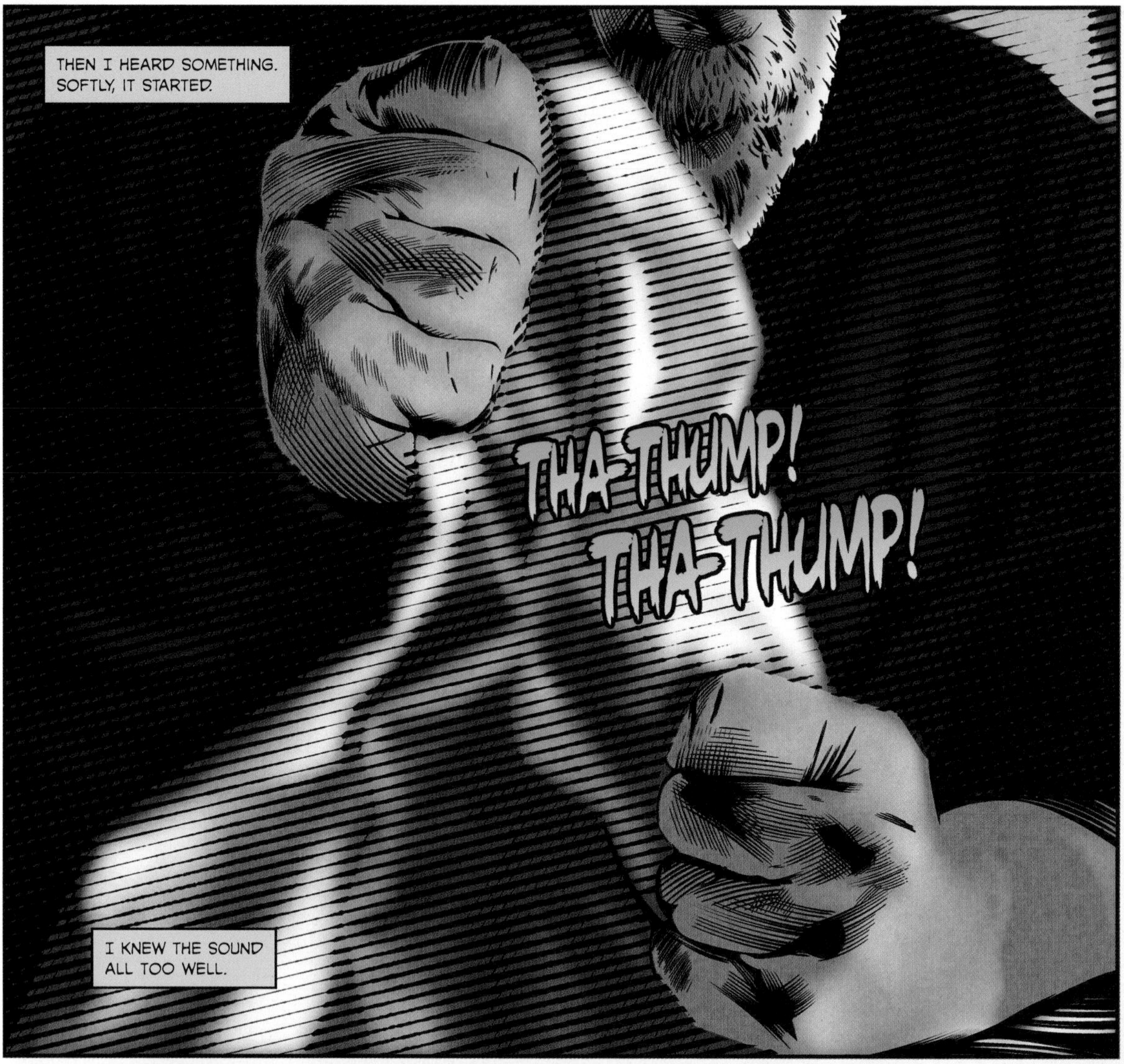
THEN I HEARD SOMETHING. SOFTLY, IT STARTED.
THA-THUMP! THA-THUMP!
I KNEW THE SOUND ALL TOO WELL.

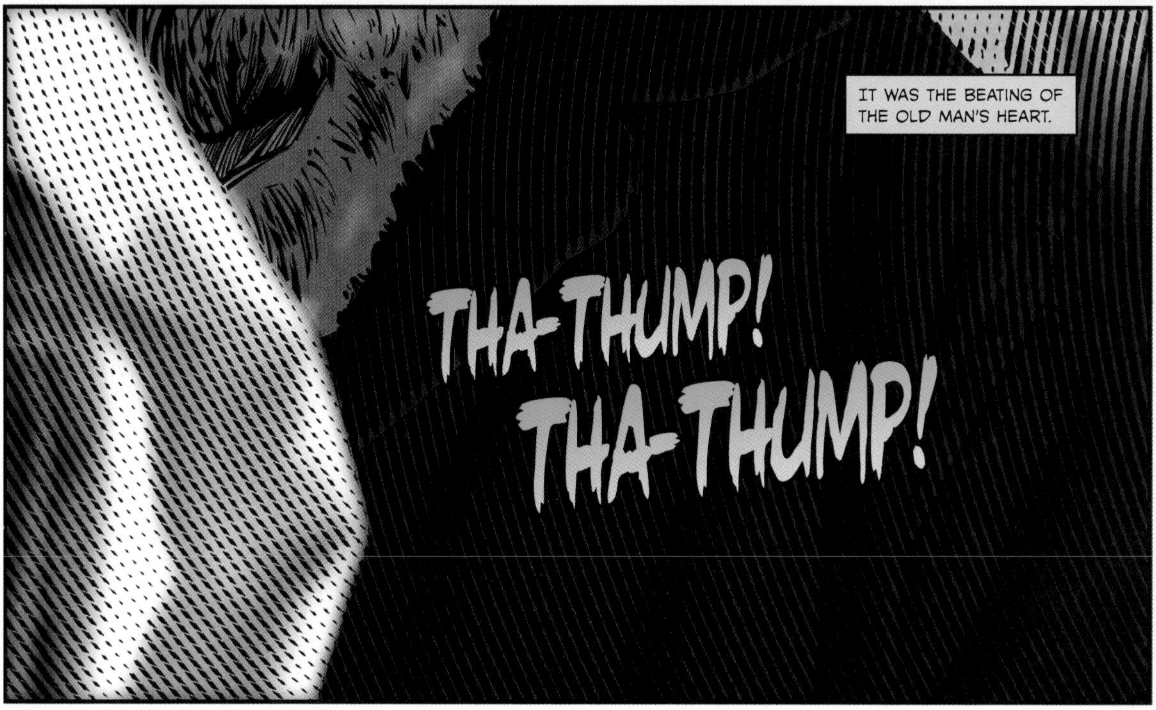
IT WAS THE BEATING OF THE OLD MAN'S HEART.
THA-THUMP! THA-THUMP!

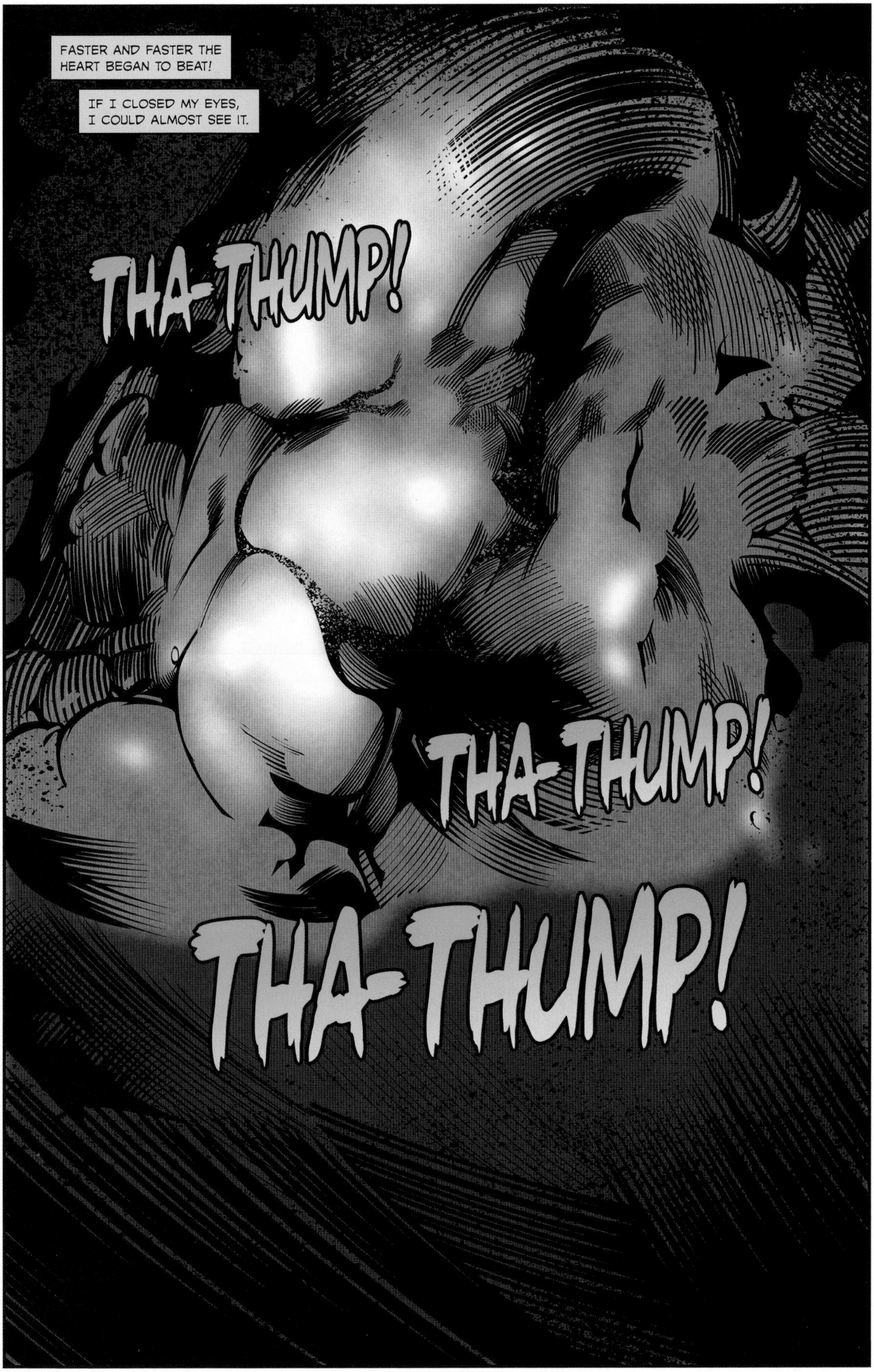
FASTER AND FASTER THE HEART BEGAN TO BEAT!
IF I CLOSED MY EYES, I COULD ALMOST SEE IT.
THA-THUMP!
THA-THUMP!
THA-THUMP!

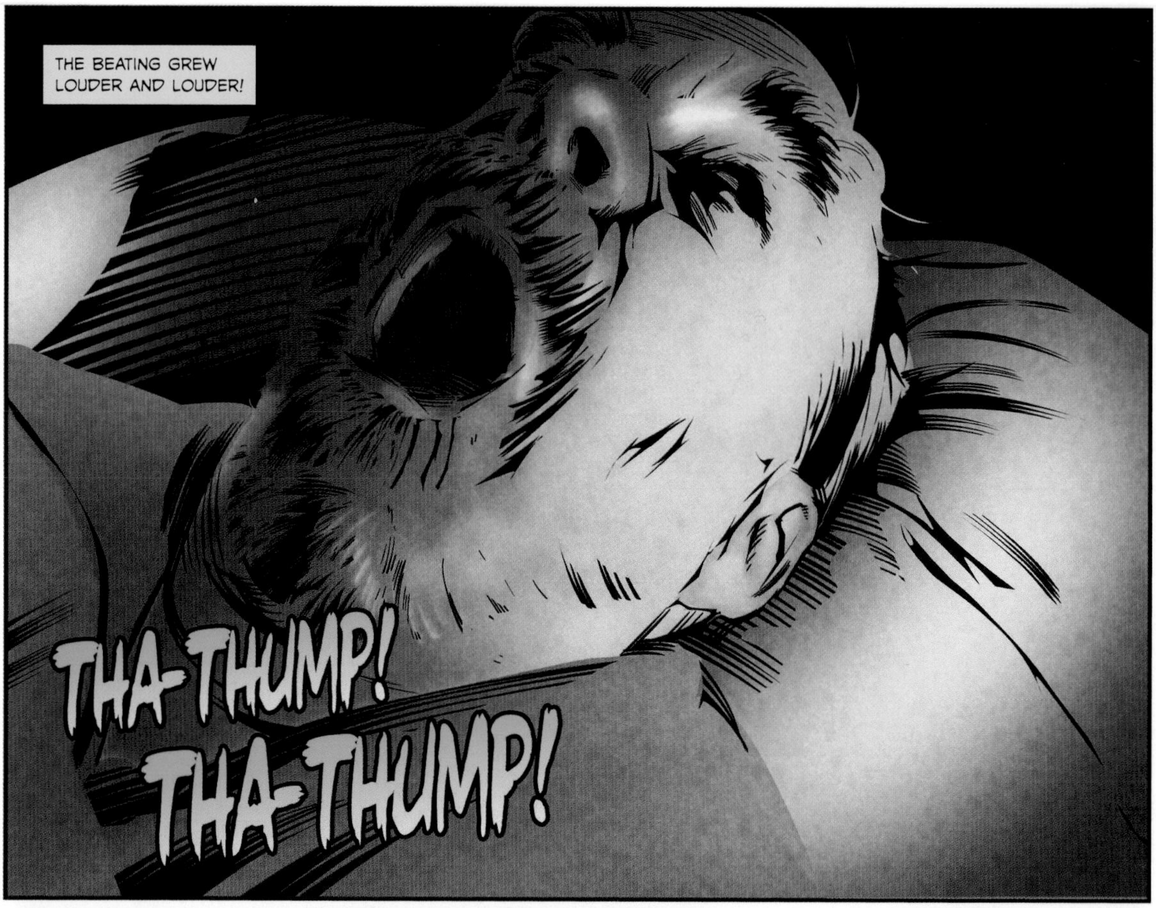
THE BEATING GREW LOUDER AND LOUDER!
THA-THUMP!
THA-THUMP!

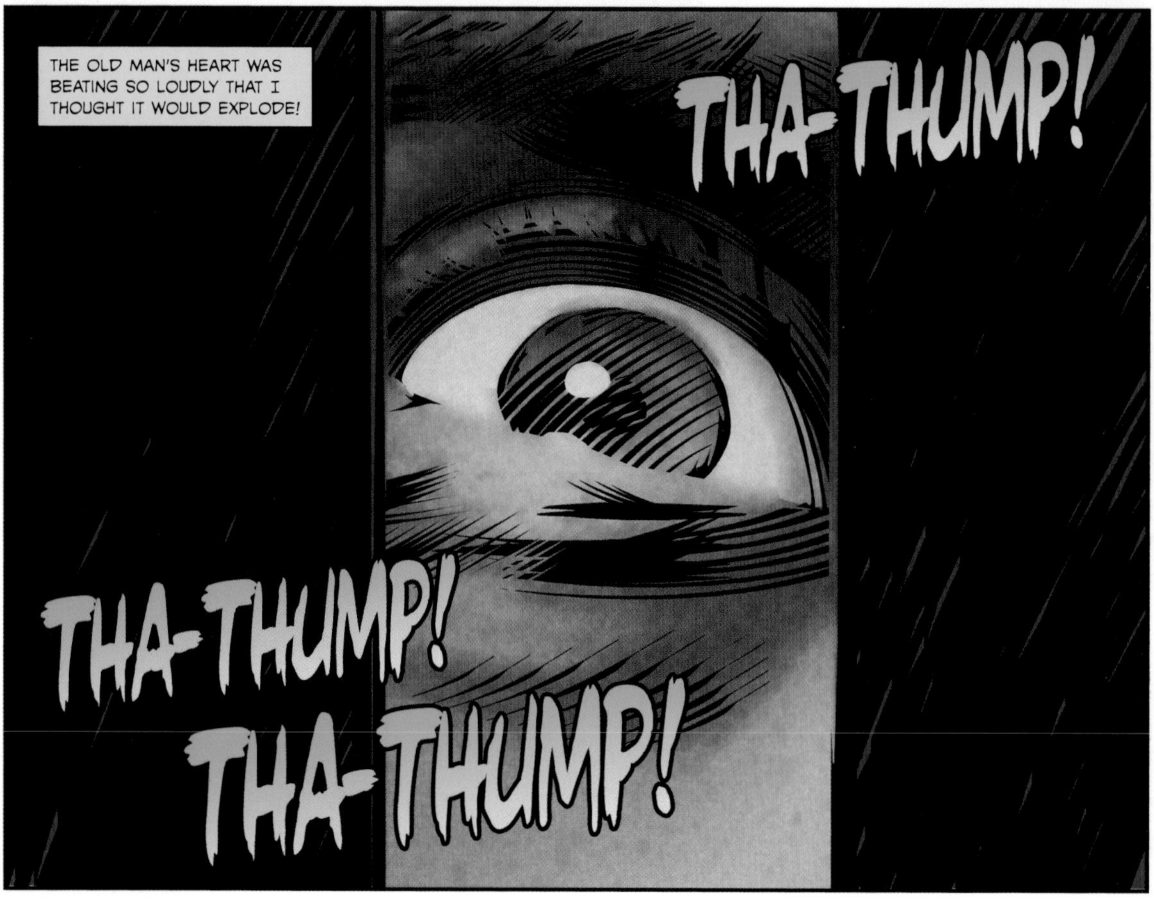
THE OLD MAN'S HEART WAS BEATING SO LOUDLY THAT I THOUGHT IT WOULD EXPLODE!
THA-THUMP!
THA-THUMP!
THA-THUMP!

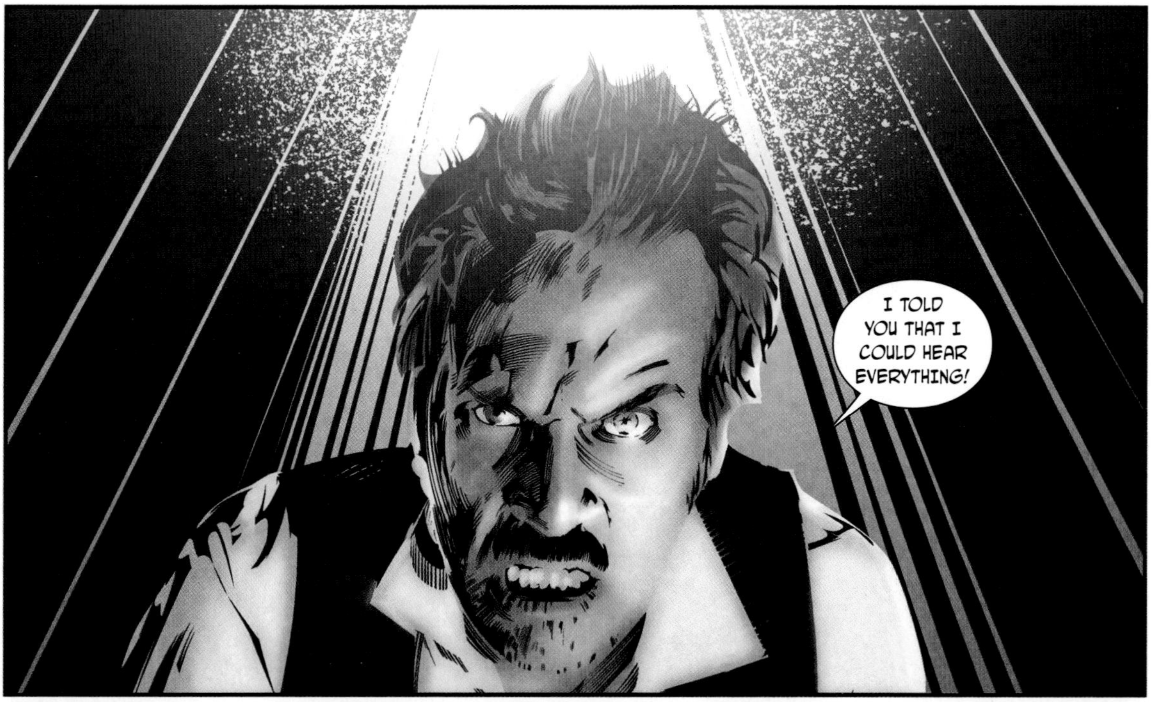
I TOLD YOU THAT I COULD HEAR EVERYTHING!

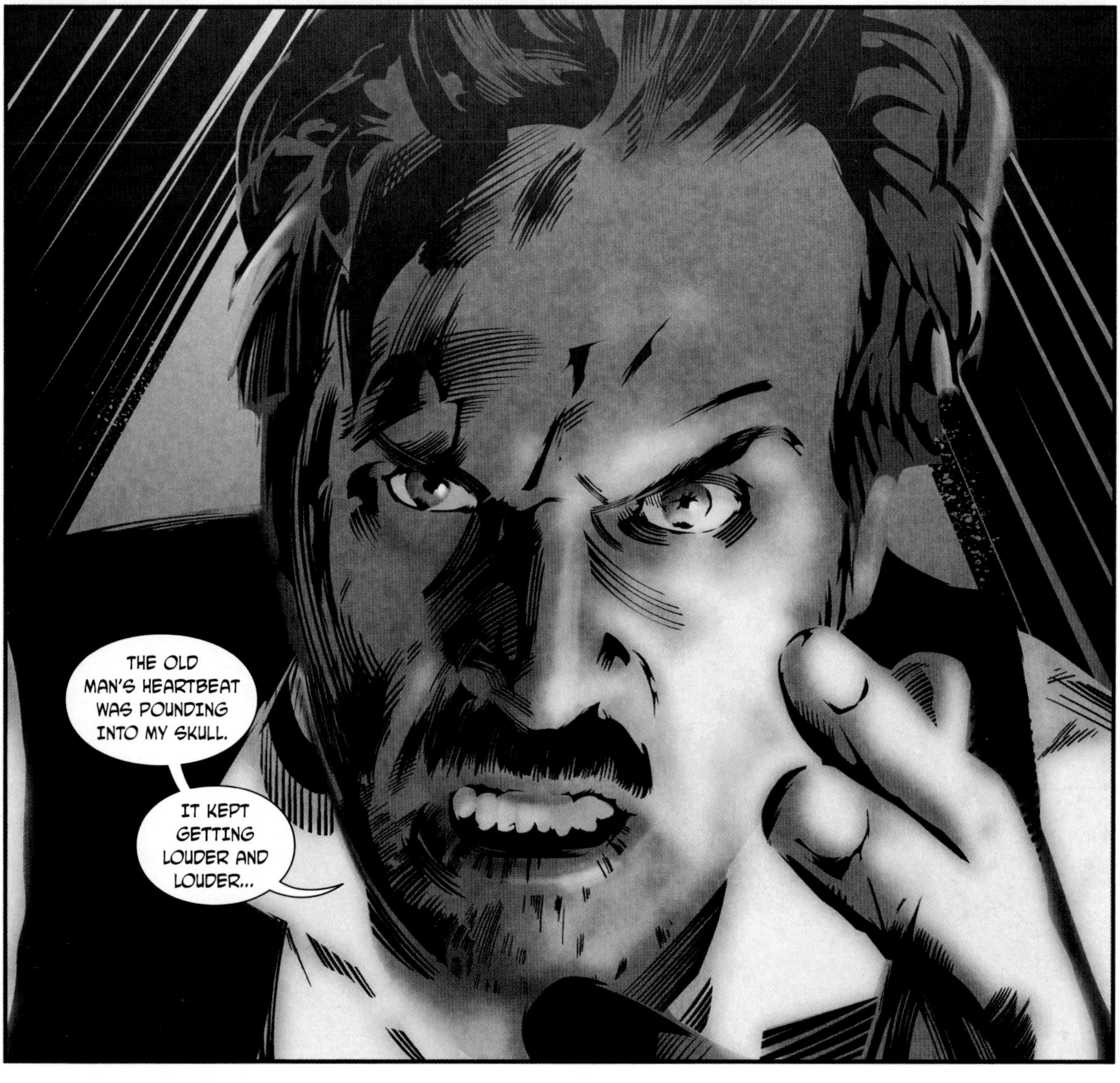
THE OLD MAN'S HEARTBEAT WAS POUNDING INTO MY SKULL.
IT KEPT GETTING LOUDER AND LOUDER...

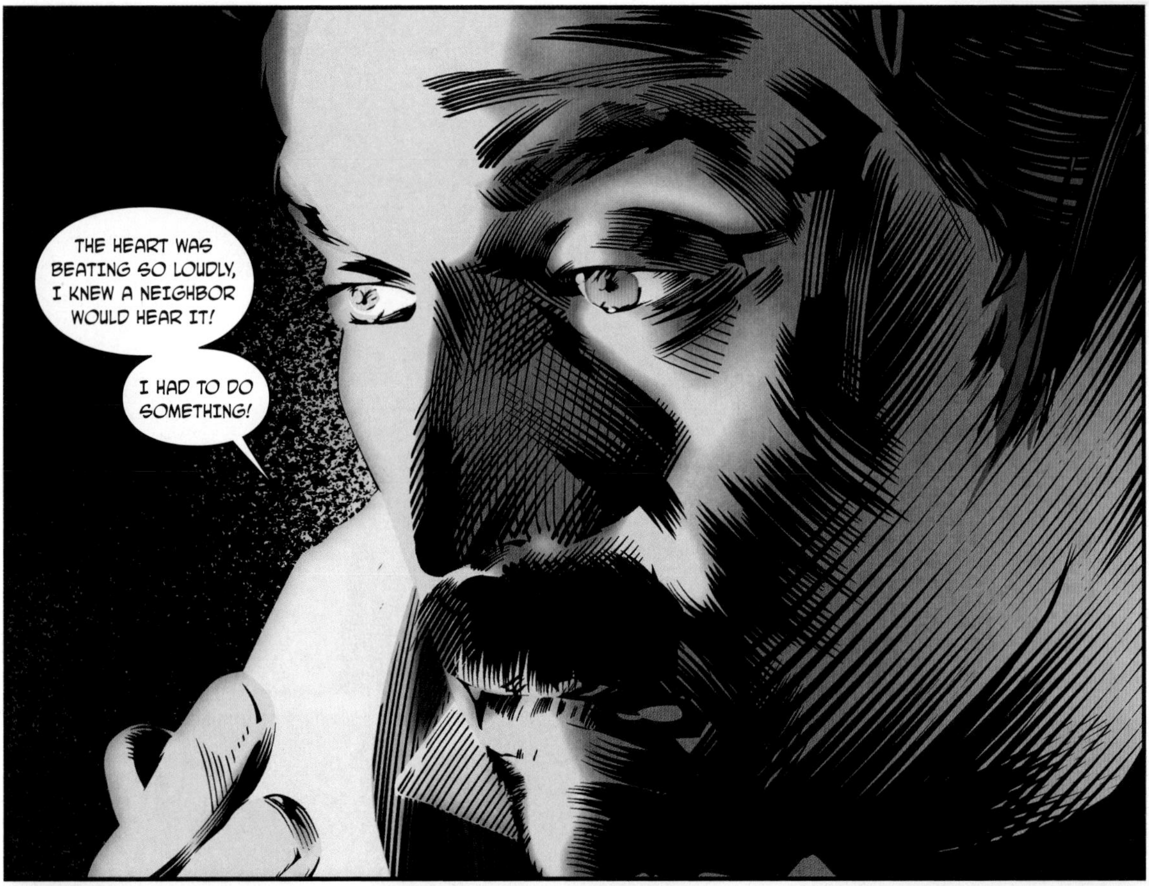
THE HEART WAS BEATING SO LOUDLY, I KNEW A NEIGHBOR WOULD HEAR IT!
I HAD TO DO SOMETHING!

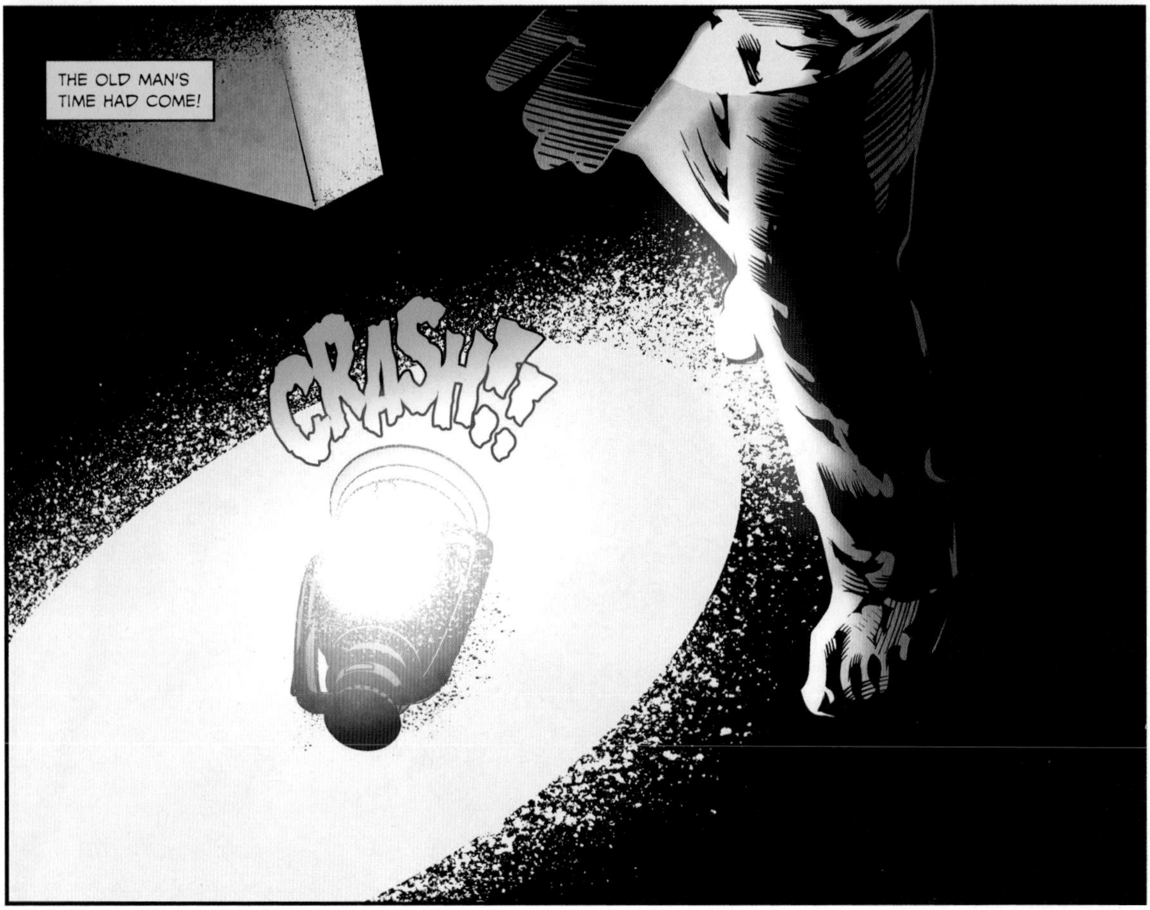
THE OLD MAN'S TIME HAD COME!
CRASH!!

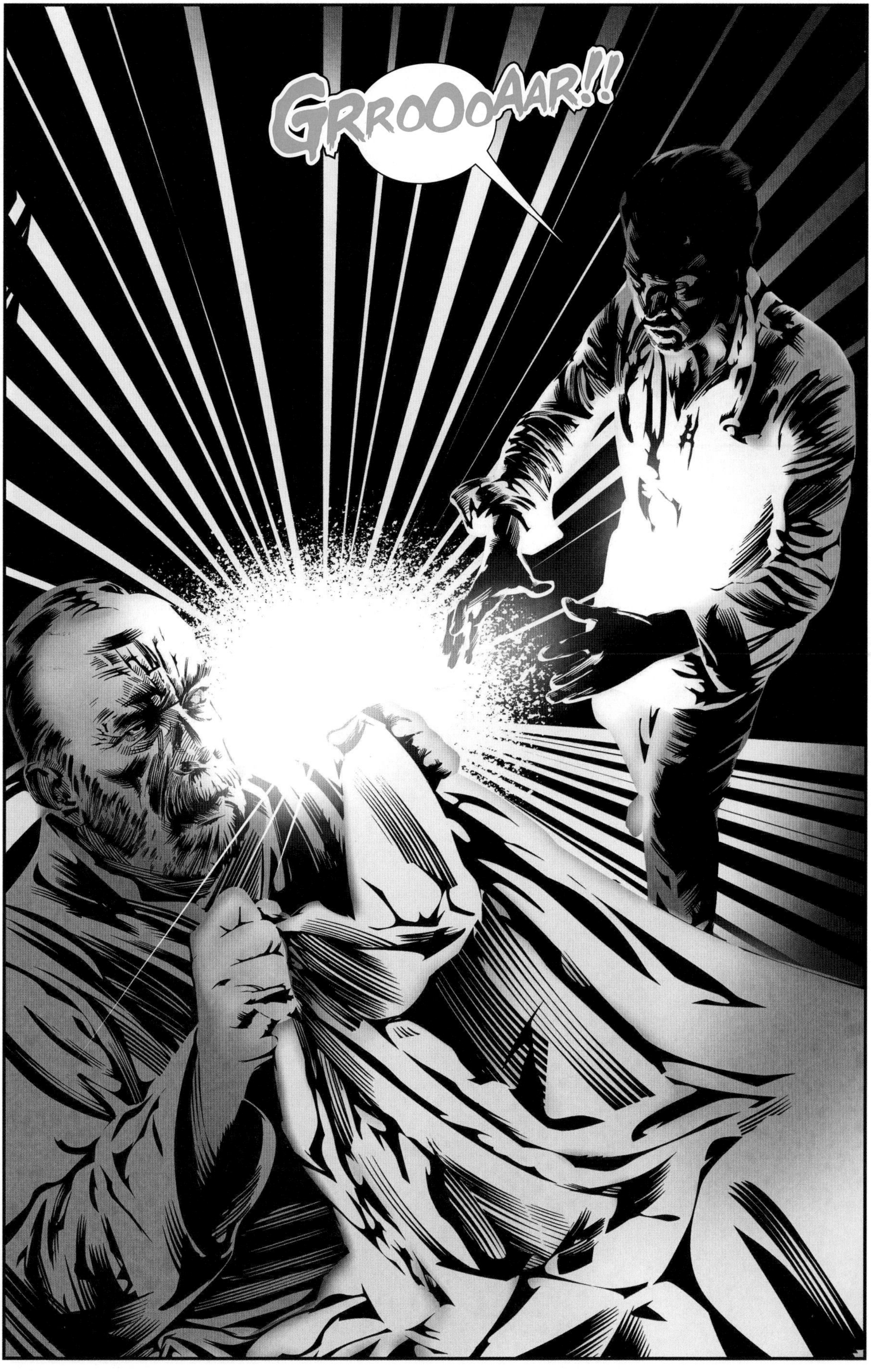
GRROOOOAAR!!

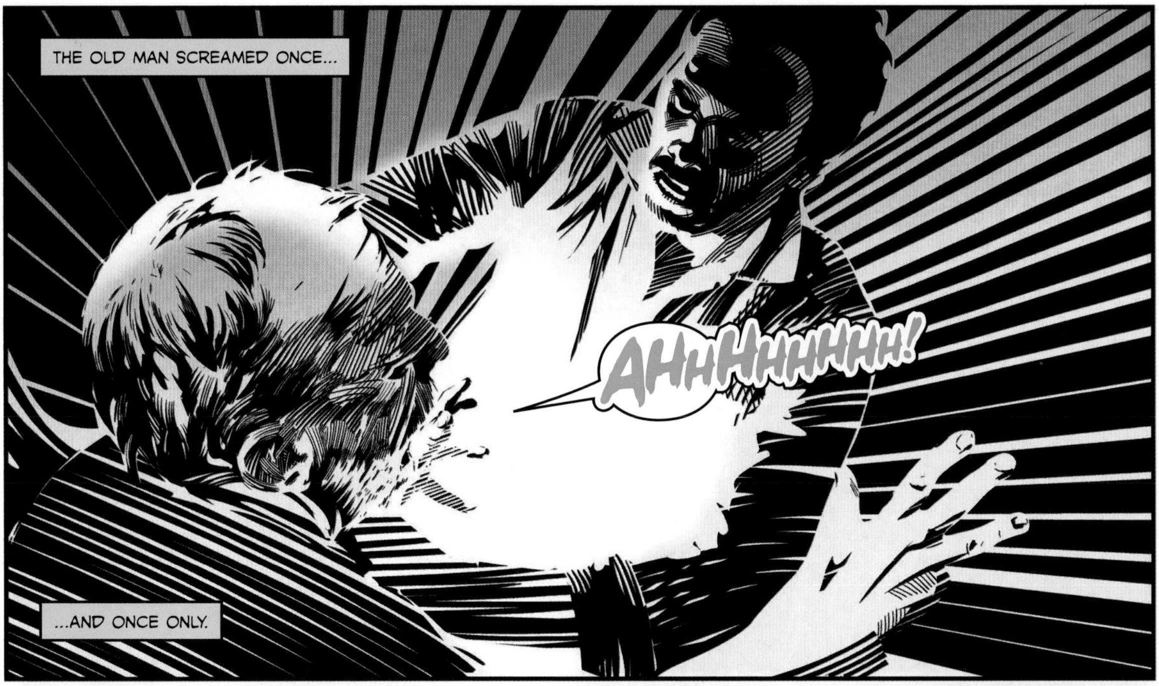
THE OLD MAN SCREAMED ONCE...
AHHHHHHHH!
...AND ONCE ONLY.

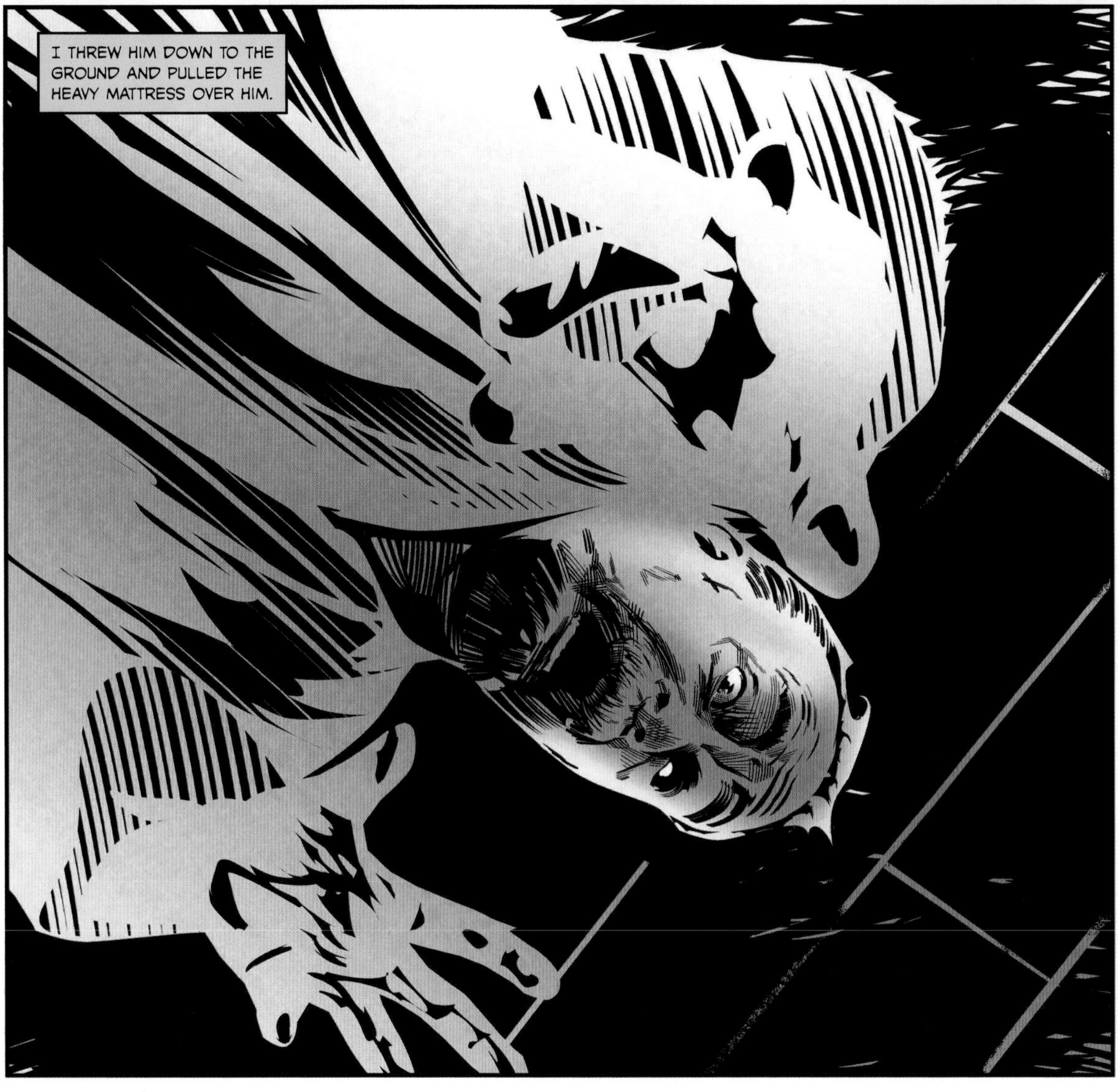
I THREW HIM DOWN TO THE GROUND AND PULLED THE HEAVY MATTRESS OVER HIM.

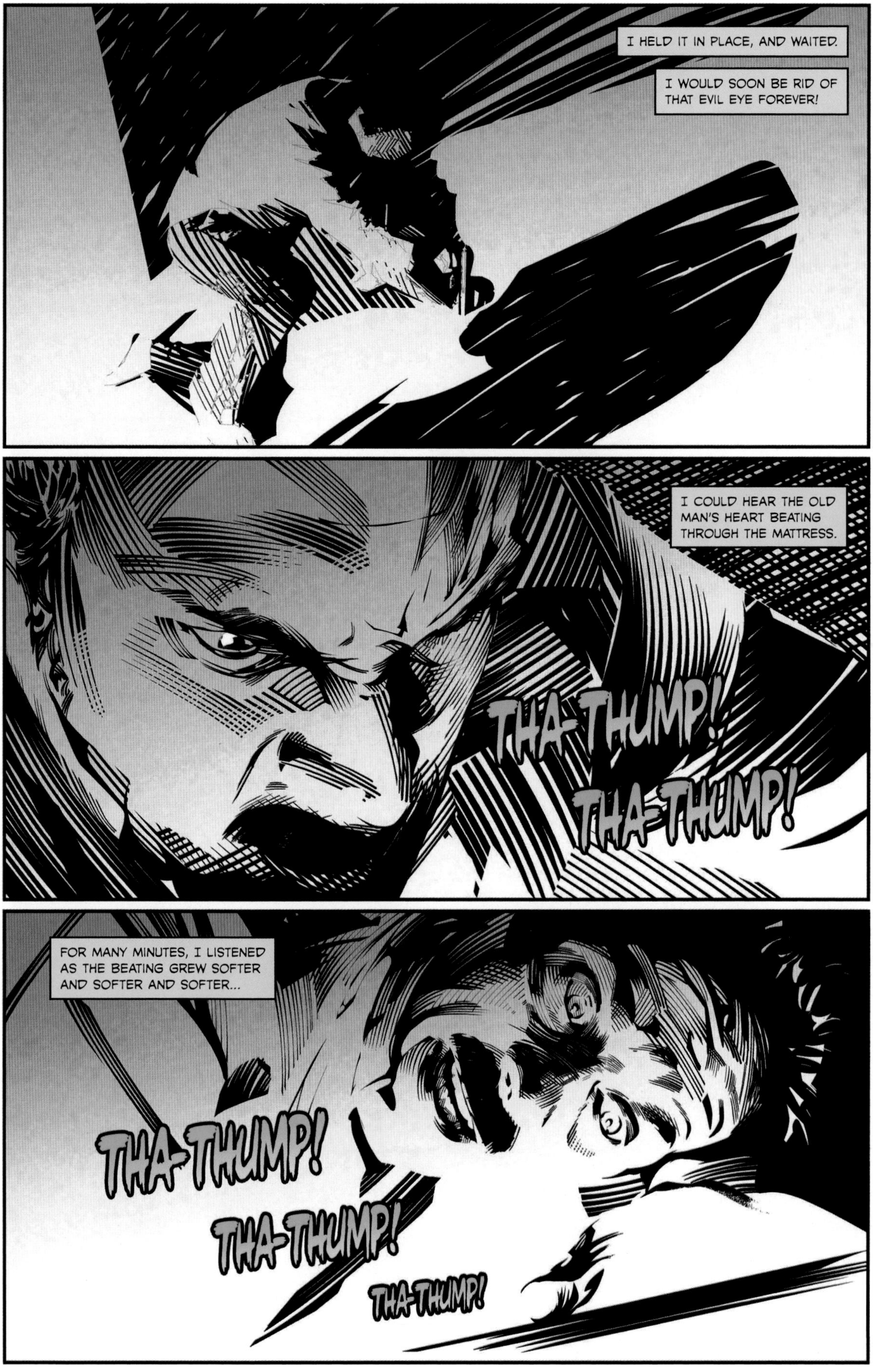
I HELD IT IN PLACE, AND WAITED.
I WOULD SOON BE RID OF THAT EVIL EYE FOREVER!
I COULD HEAR THE OLD MAN'S HEART BEATING THROUGH THE MATTRESS.
THA-THUMP!
THA-THUMP!
FOR MANY MINUTES, I LISTENED AS THE BEATING GREW SOFTER AND SOFTER AND SOFTER...
THA-THUMP!
THA-THUMP!
THA-THUMP!

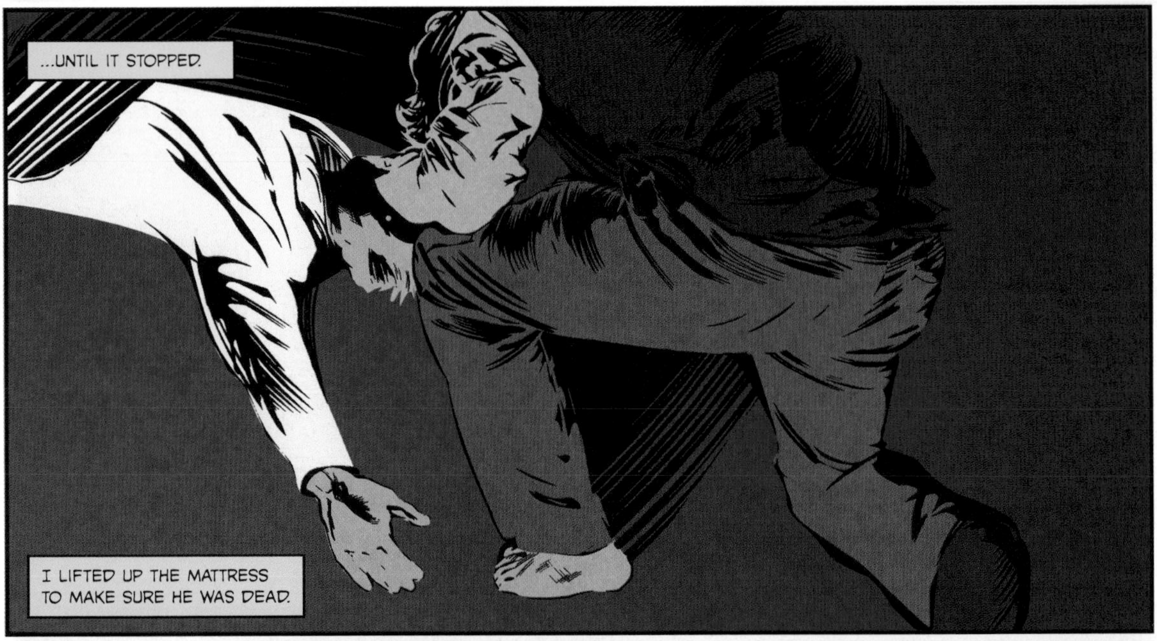
...UNTIL IT STOPPED.
I LIFTED UP THE MATTRESS TO MAKE SURE HE WAS DEAD.

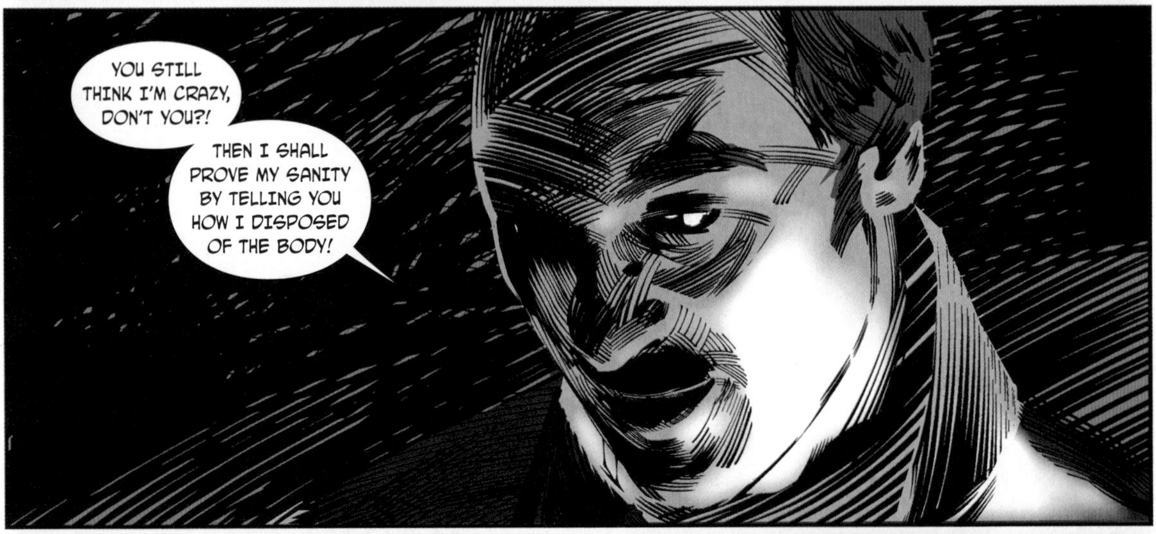
YOU STILL THINK I'M CRAZY, DON'T YOU?!
THEN I SHALL PROVE MY SANITY BY TELLING YOU HOW I DISPOSED OF THE BODY!

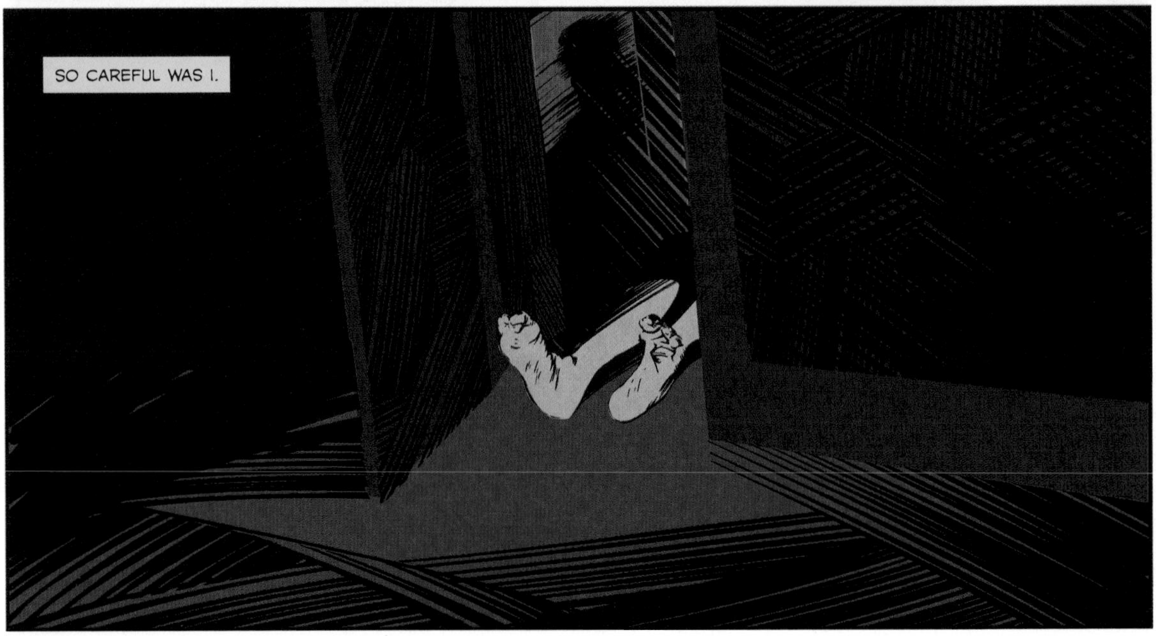
SO CAREFUL WAS I.

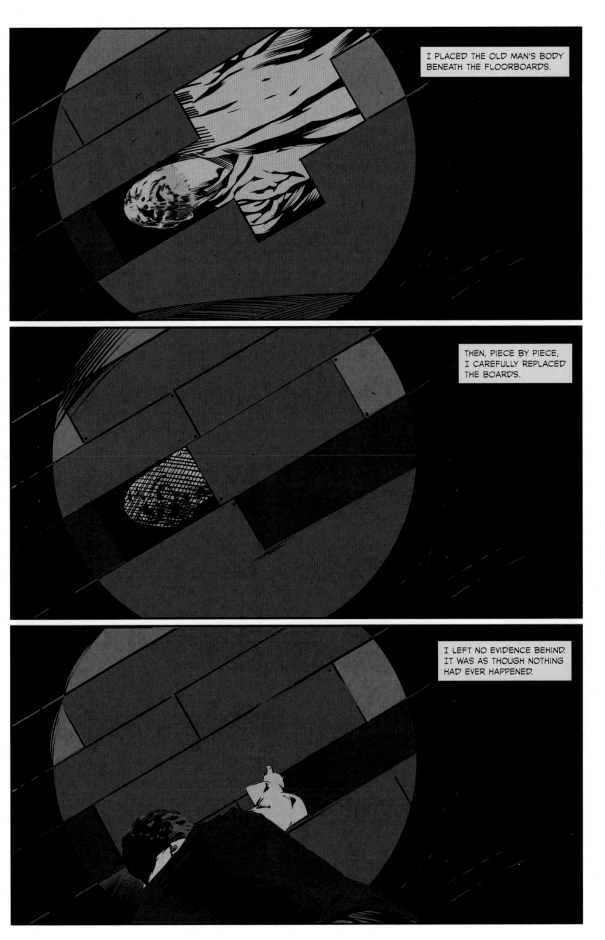

I PLACED THE OLD MAN'S BODY BENEATH THE FLOORBOARDS.

THEN, PIECE BY PIECE, I CAREFULLY REPLACED THE BOARDS.

I LEFT NO EVIDENCE BEHIND. IT WAS AS THOUGH NOTHING HAD EVER HAPPENED.

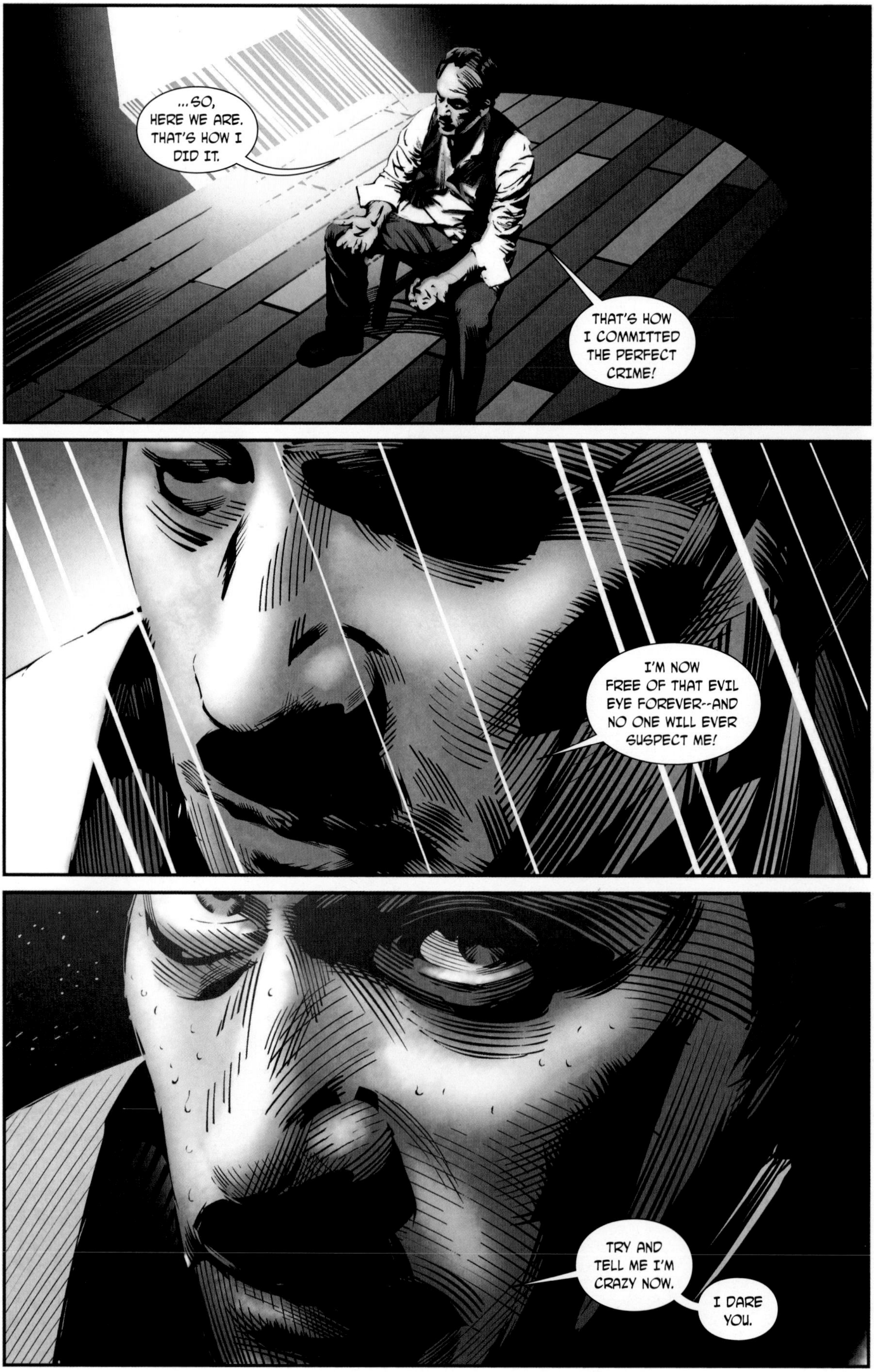
...SO, HERE WE ARE. THAT'S HOW I DID IT.
THAT'S HOW I COMMITTED THE PERFECT CRIME!
I'M NOW FREE OF THAT EVIL EYE FOREVER--AND NO ONE WILL EVER SUSPECT ME!
TRY AND TELL ME I'M CRAZY NOW.
I DARE YOU.

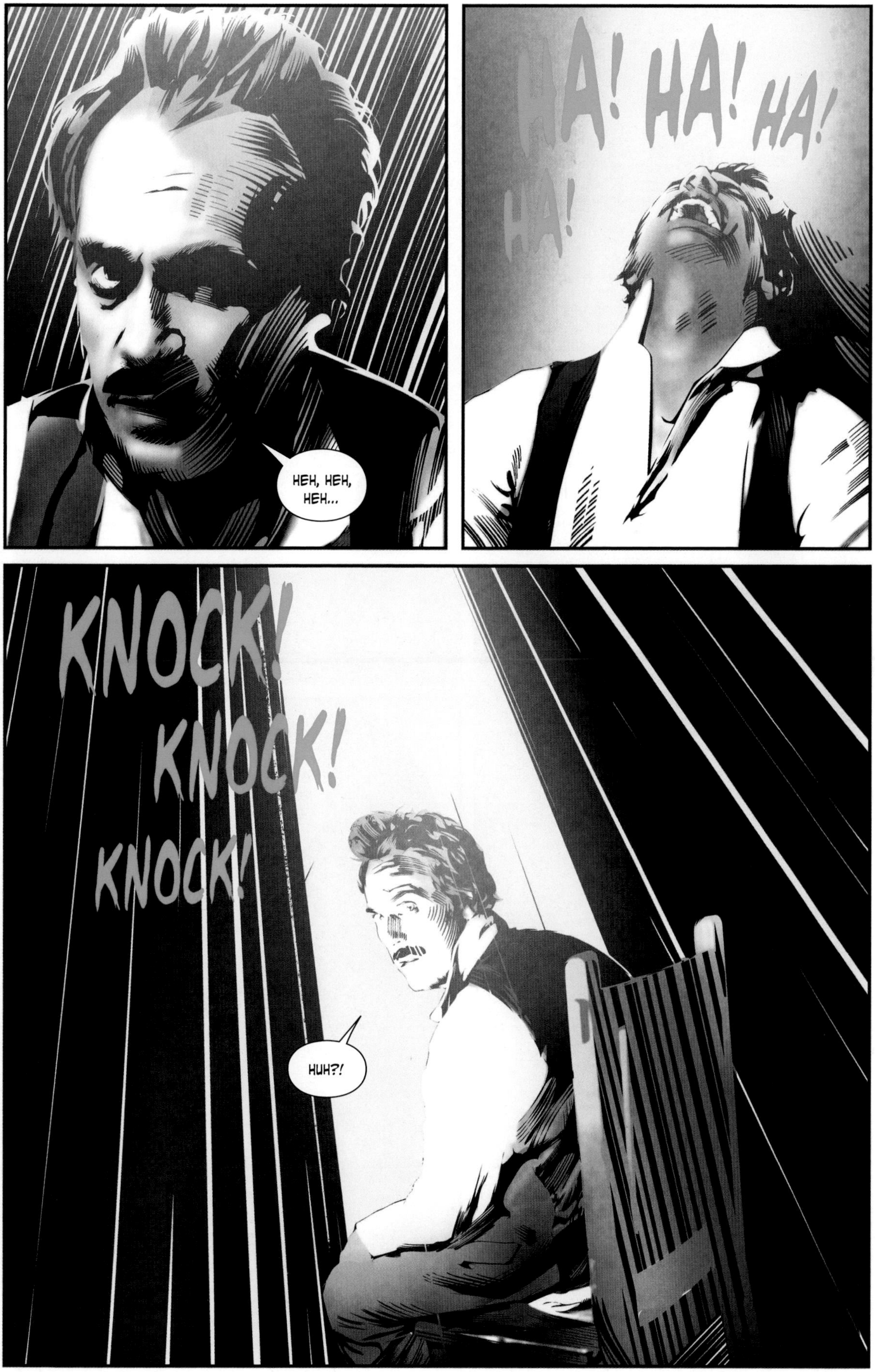
HEH, HEH, HEH...
HA! HA! HA! HA!
KNOCK! KNOCK! KNOCK!
HUH?!

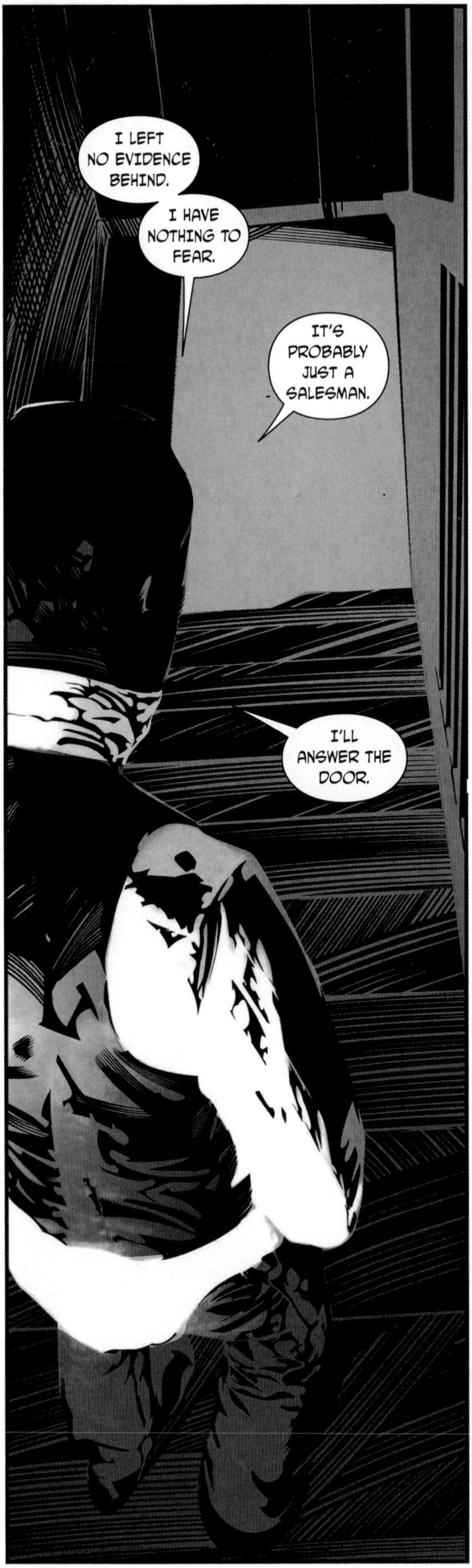
I LEFT NO EVIDENCE BEHIND.
I HAVE NOTHING TO FEAR.
IT'S PROBABLY JUST A SALESMAN.
I'LL ANSWER THE DOOR.

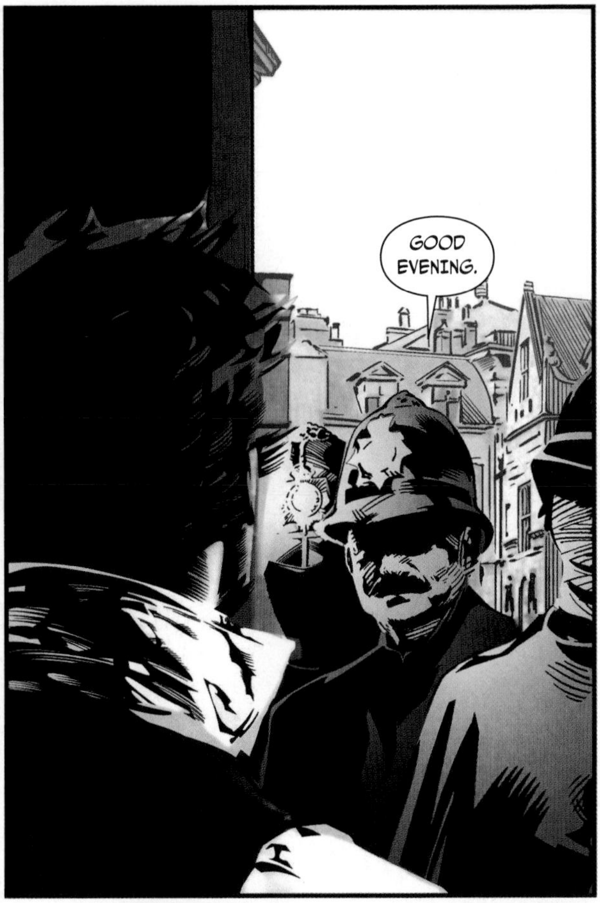
GOOD EVENING.

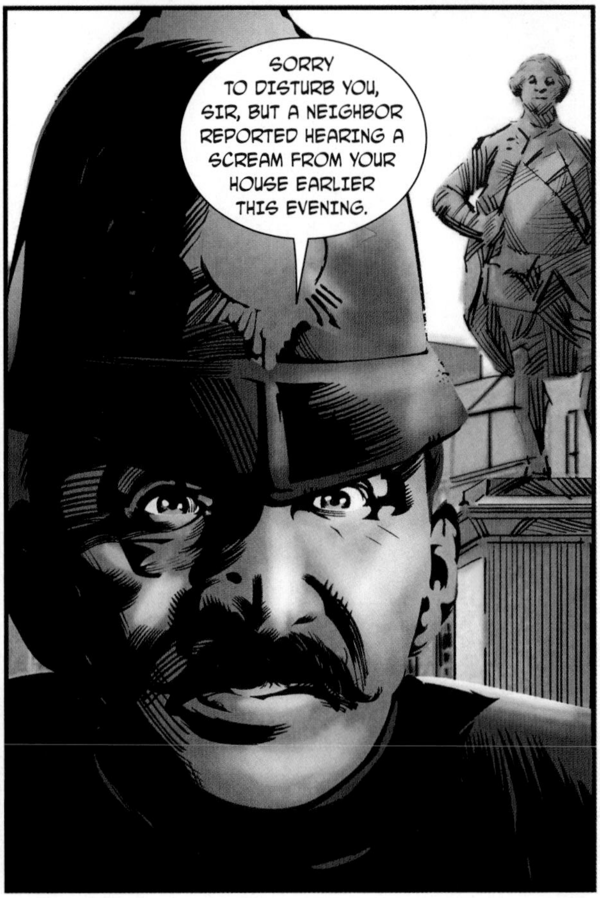
SORRY TO DISTURB YOU, SIR, BUT A NEIGHBOR REPORTED HEARING A SCREAM FROM YOUR HOUSE EARLIER THIS EVENING.

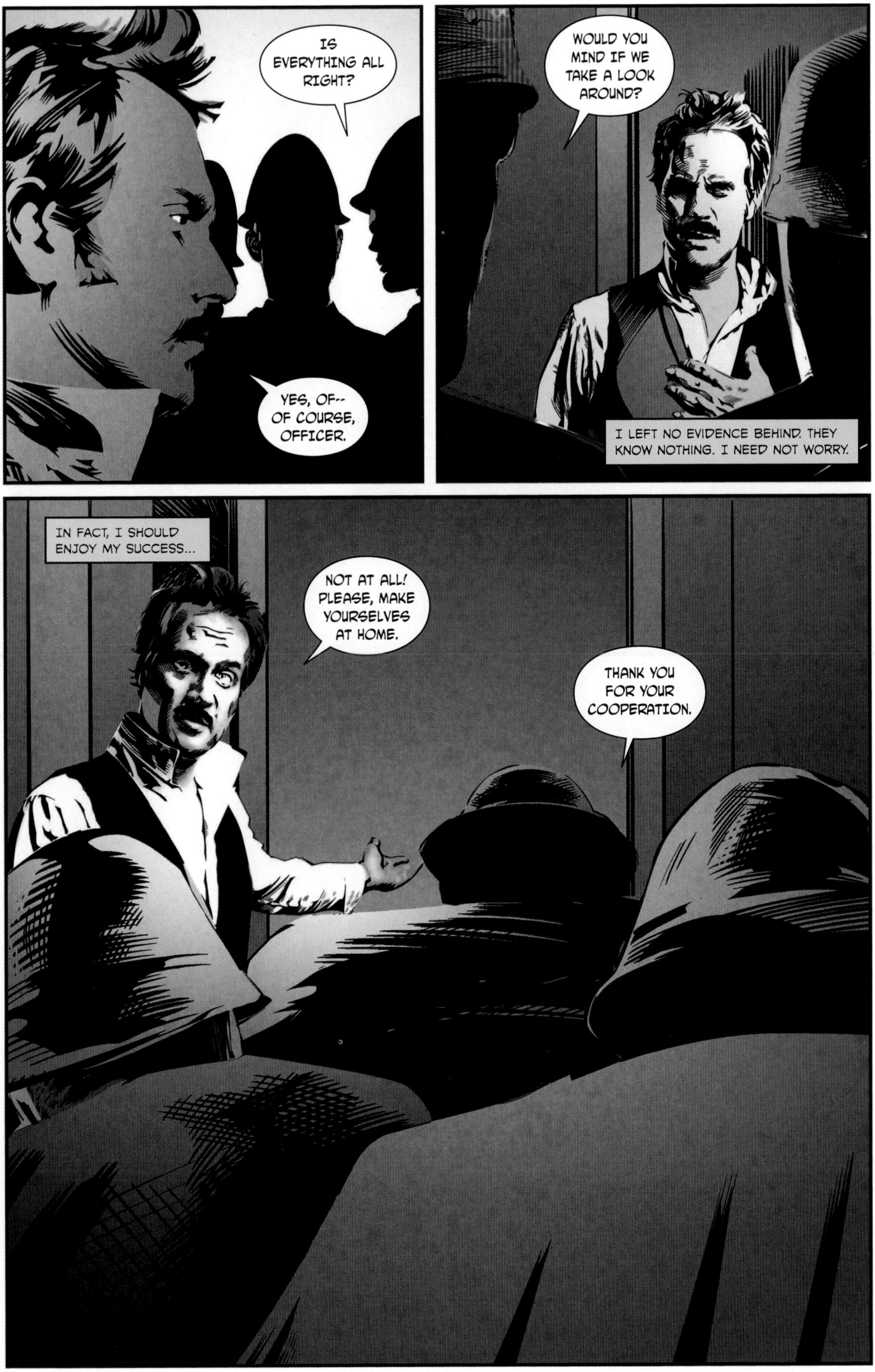
IS EVERYTHING ALL RIGHT?
YES, OF-- OF COURSE, OFFICER.
WOULD YOU MIND IF WE TAKE A LOOK AROUND?
I LEFT NO EVIDENCE BEHIND. THEY KNOW NOTHING. I NEED NOT WORRY.
IN FACT, I SHOULD ENJOY MY SUCCESS...
NOT AT ALL! PLEASE, MAKE YOURSELVES AT HOME.
THANK YOU FOR YOUR COOPERATION.

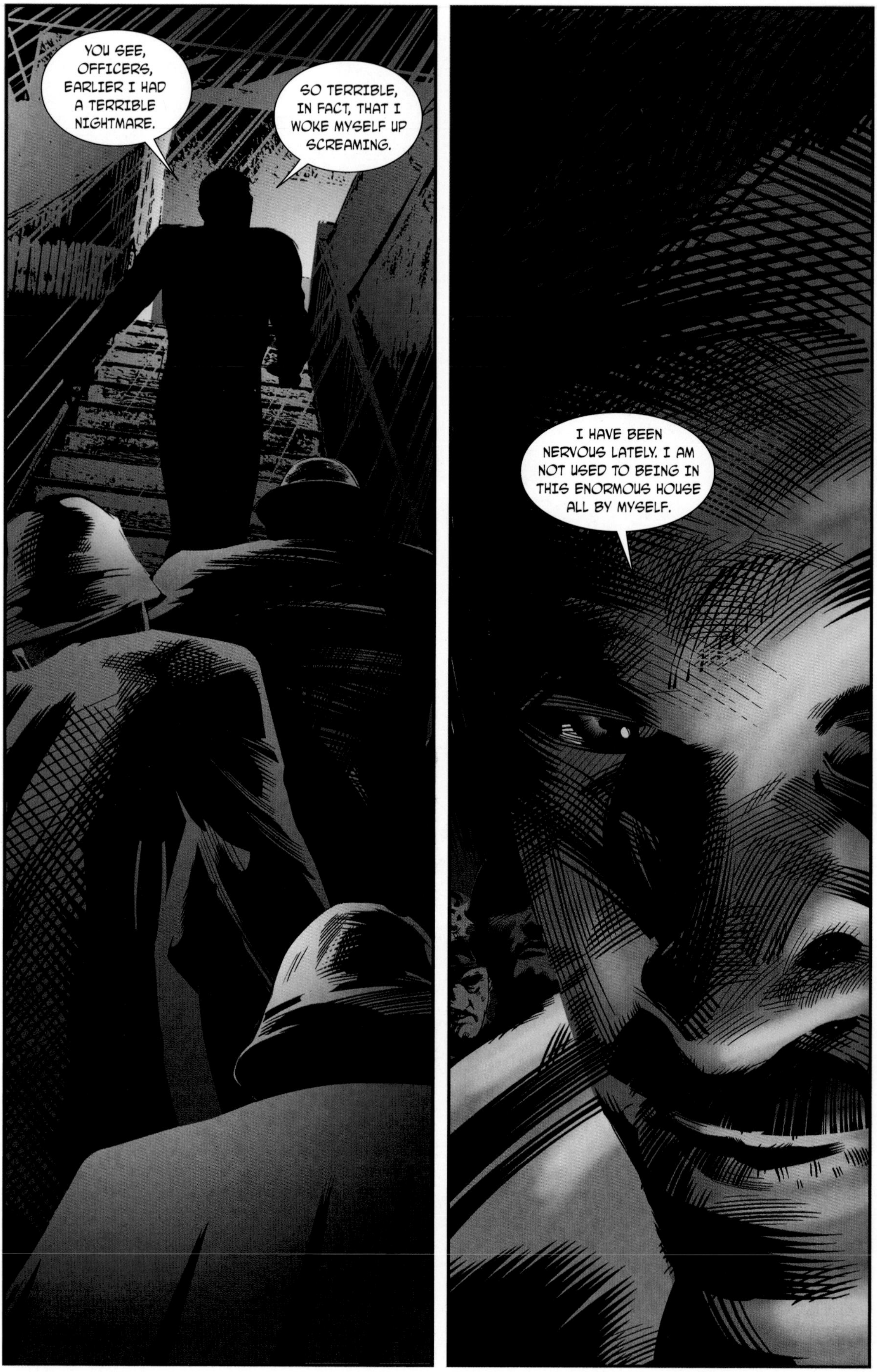
YOU SEE, OFFICERS, EARLIER I HAD A TERRIBLE NIGHTMARE.
SO TERRIBLE, IN FACT, THAT I WOKE MYSELF UP SCREAMING.
I HAVE BEEN NERVOUS LATELY. I AM NOT USED TO BEING IN THIS ENORMOUS HOUSE ALL BY MYSELF.

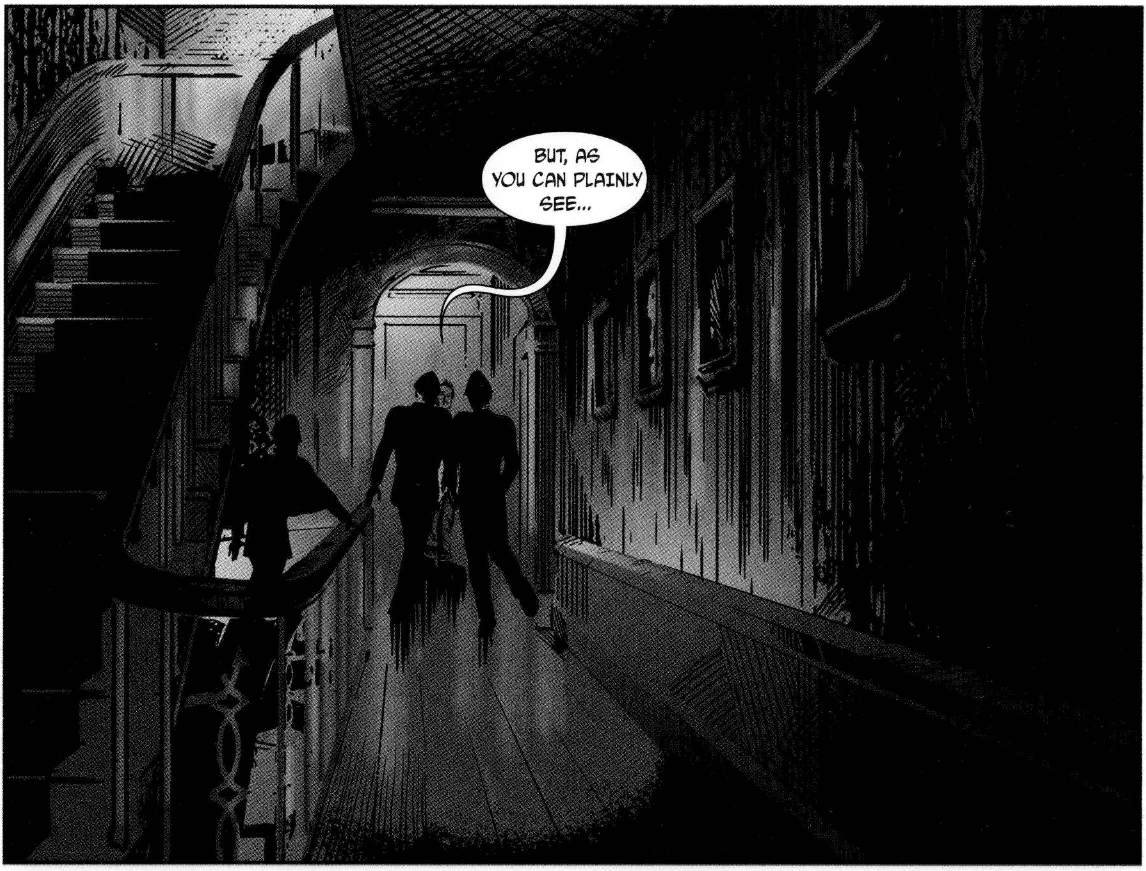
BUT, AS YOU CAN PLAINLY SEE...

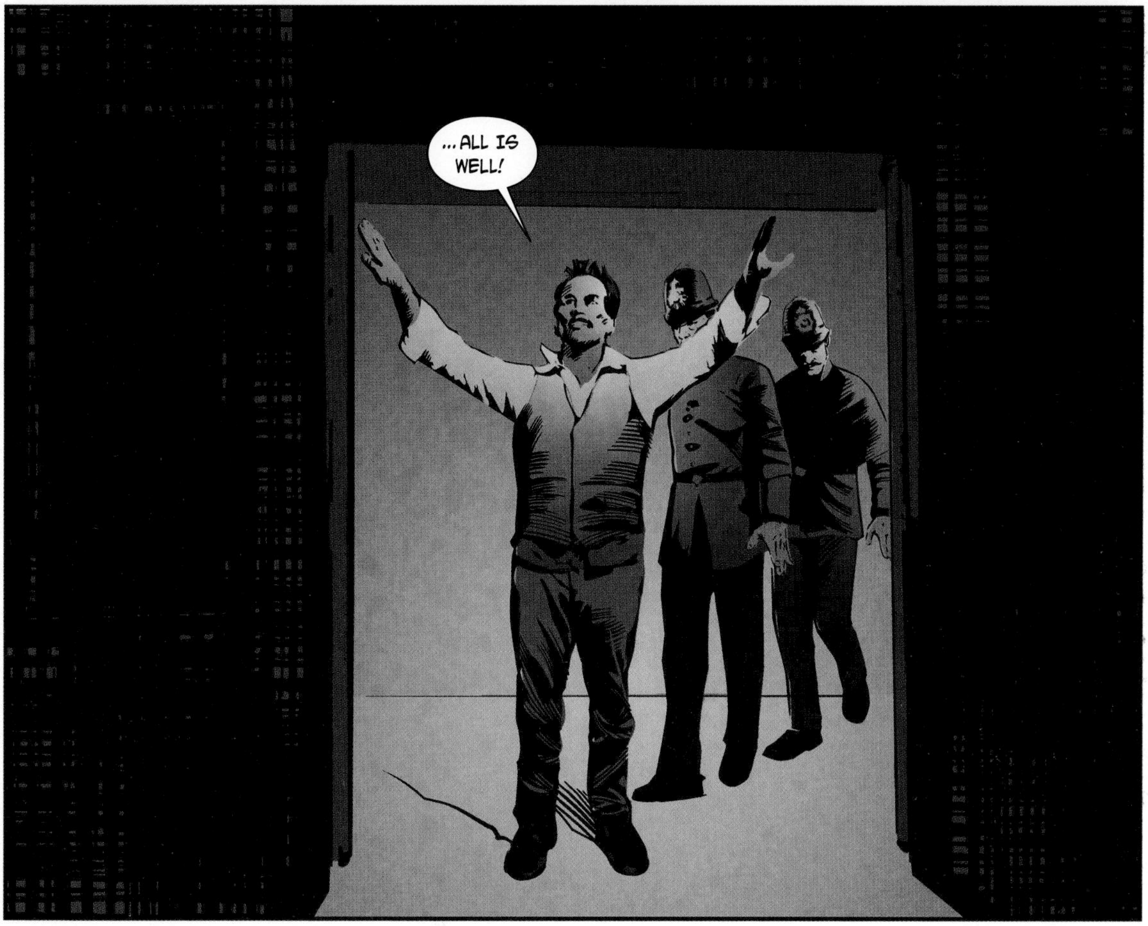
...ALL IS WELL!

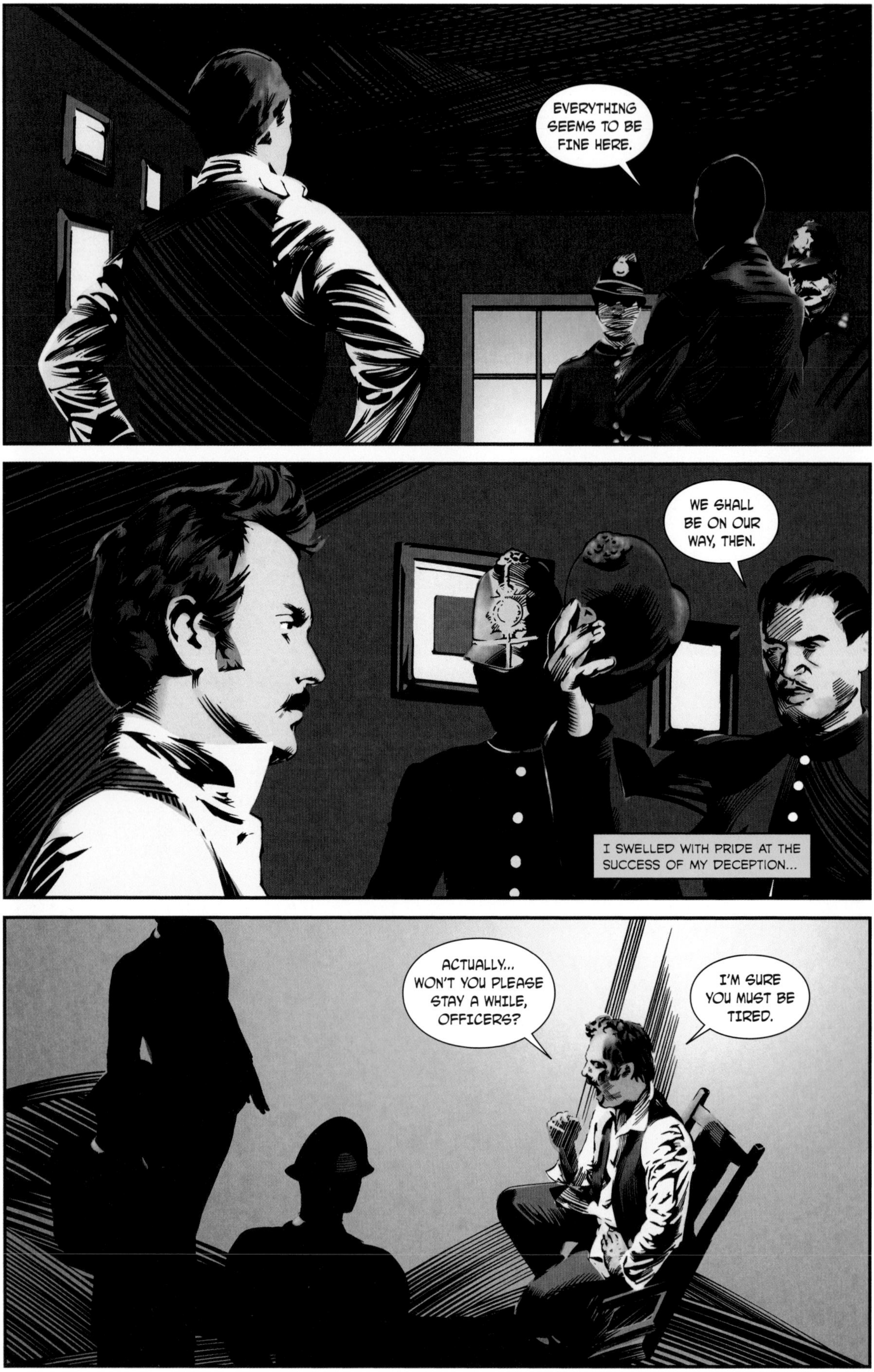
EVERYTHING SEEMS TO BE FINE HERE.
WE SHALL BE ON OUR WAY, THEN.
I SWELLED WITH PRIDE AT THE SUCCESS OF MY DECEPTION...
ACTUALLY... WON'T YOU PLEASE STAY A WHILE, OFFICERS?
I'M SURE YOU MUST BE TIRED.

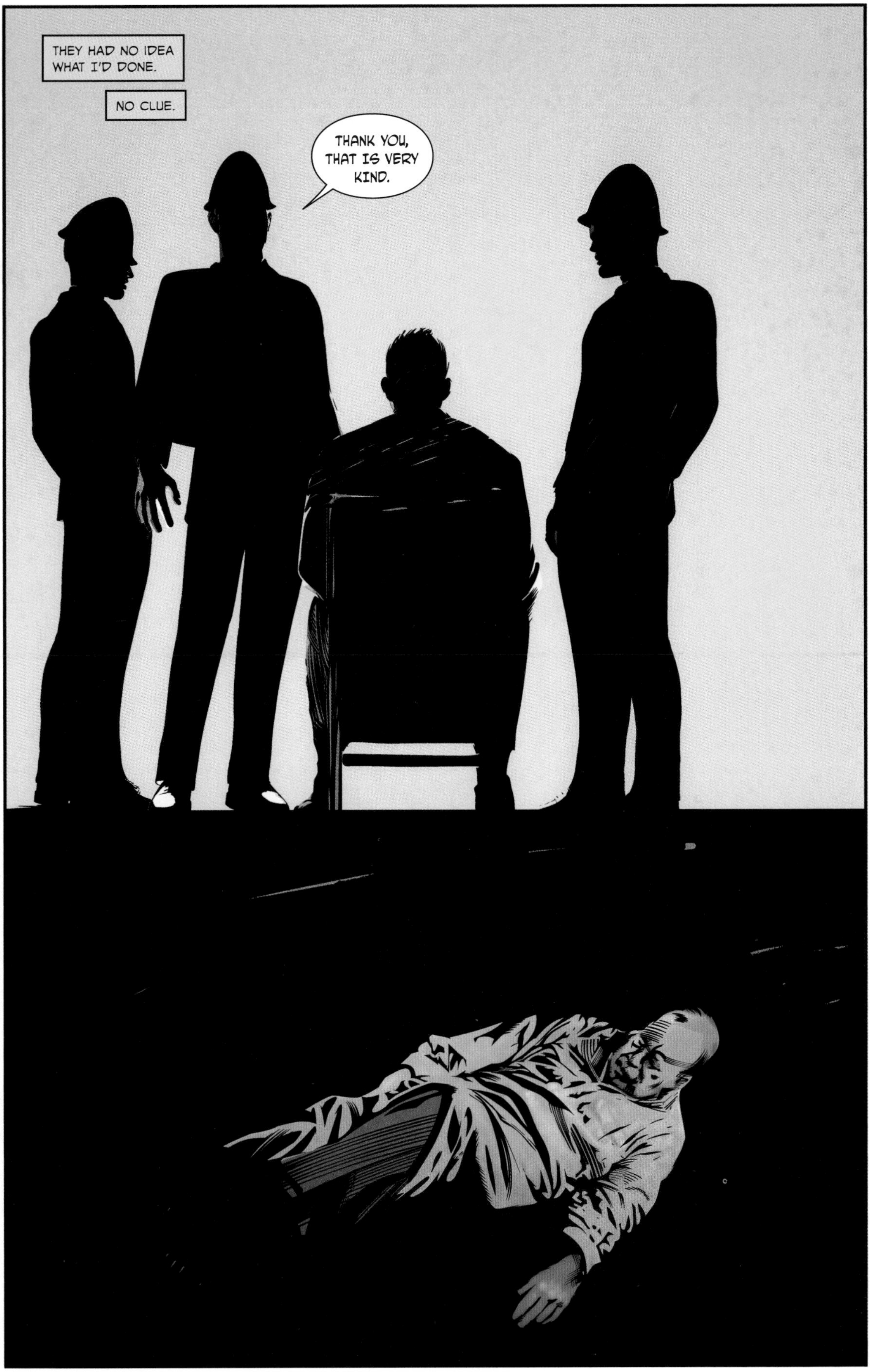
THEY HAD NO IDEA WHAT I'D DONE.
NO CLUE.
THANK YOU, THAT IS VERY KIND.

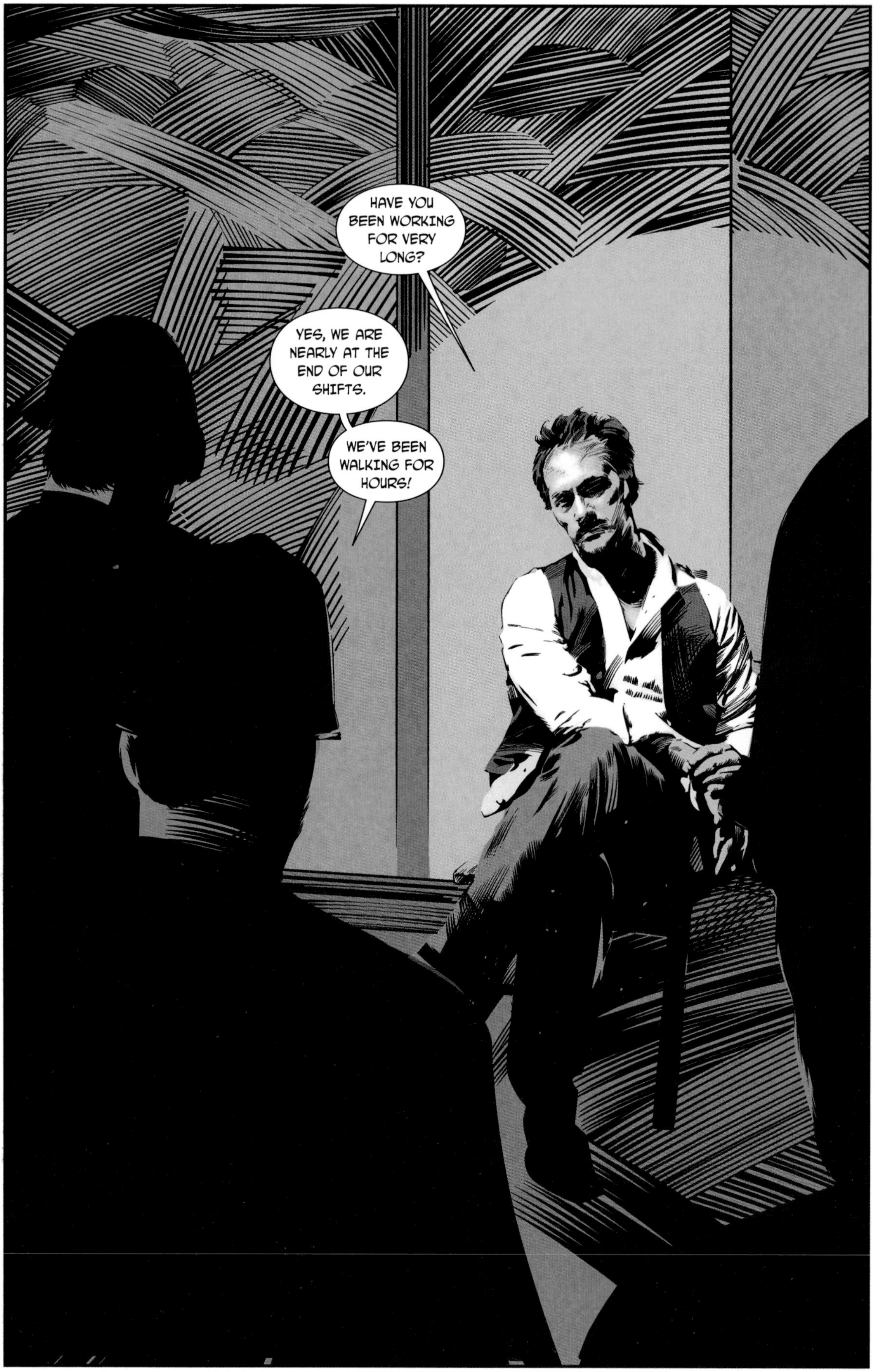
HAVE YOU BEEN WORKING FOR VERY LONG?
YES, WE ARE NEARLY AT THE END OF OUR SHIFTS.
WE'VE BEEN WALKING FOR HOURS!

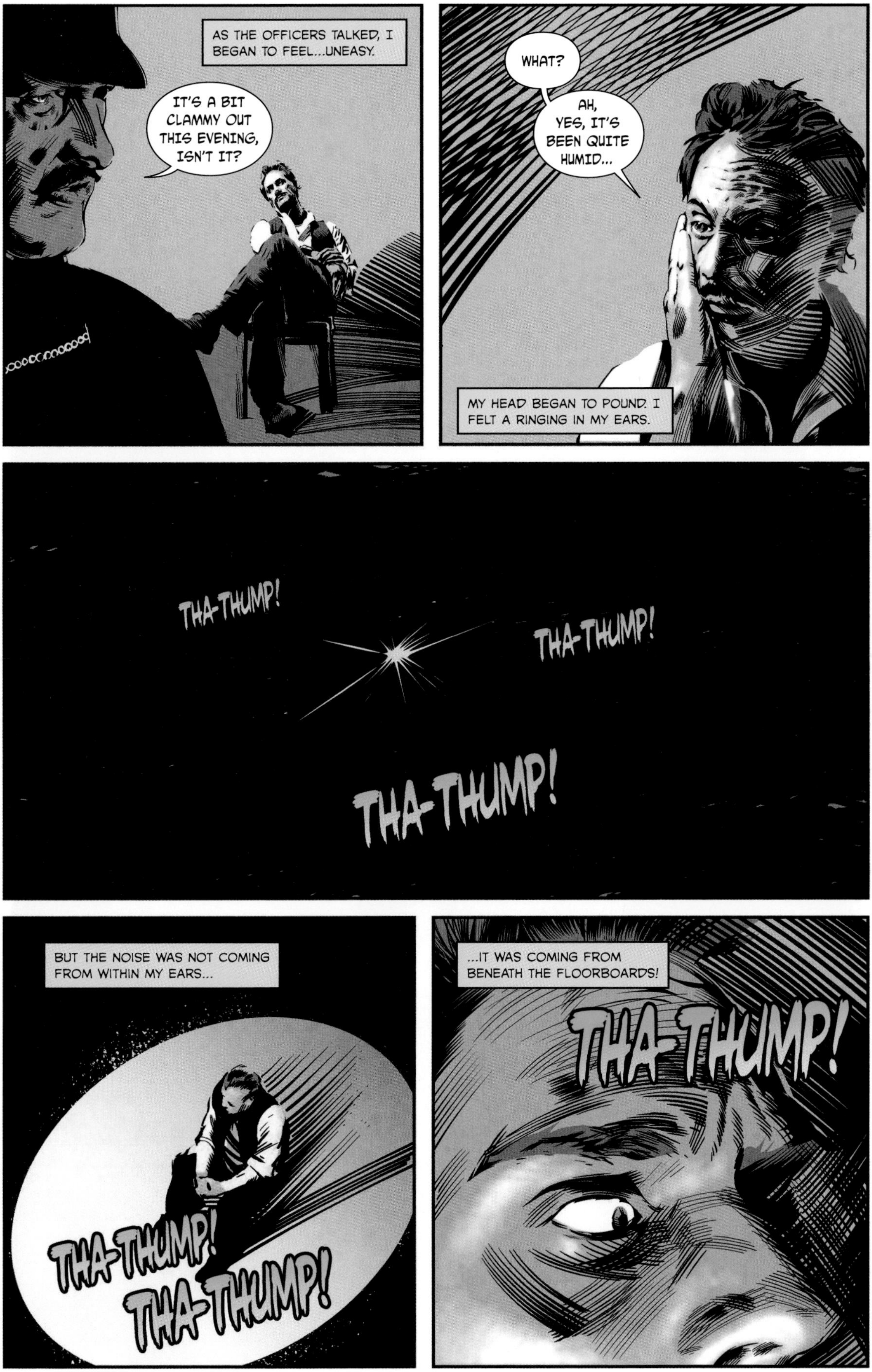
AS THE OFFICERS TALKED, I BEGAN TO FEEL...UNEASY.
IT'S A BIT CLAMMY OUT THIS EVENING, ISN'T IT?
WHAT?
AH, YES, IT'S BEEN QUITE HUMID...
MY HEAD BEGAN TO POUND. I FELT A RINGING IN MY EARS.
THA-THUMP!
THA-THUMP!
THA-THUMP!
BUT THE NOISE WAS NOT COMING FROM WITHIN MY EARS...
THA-THUMP!
THA-THUMP!
...IT WAS COMING FROM BENEATH THE FLOORBOARDS!
THA-THUMP!

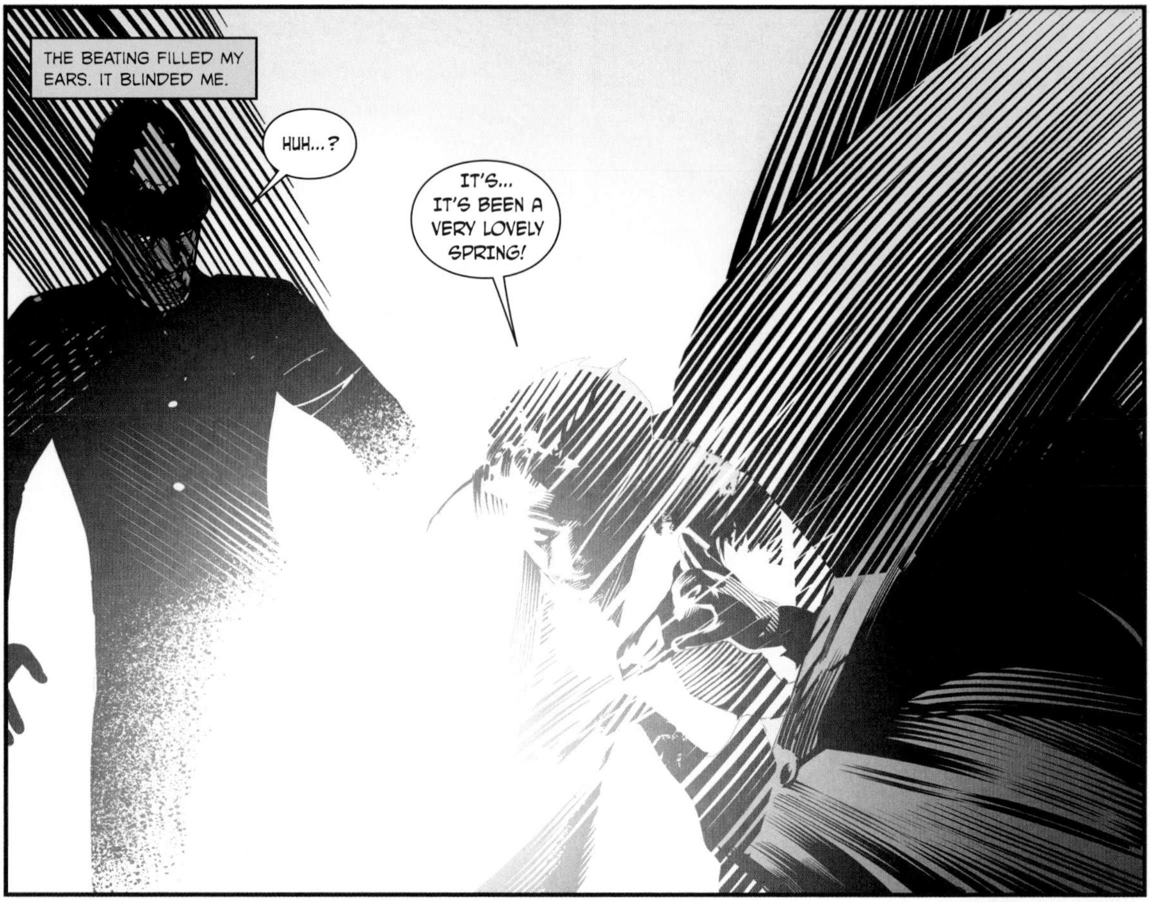
THE BEATING FILLED MY EARS. IT BLINDED ME.
HUH...?
IT'S... IT'S BEEN A VERY LOVELY SPRING!

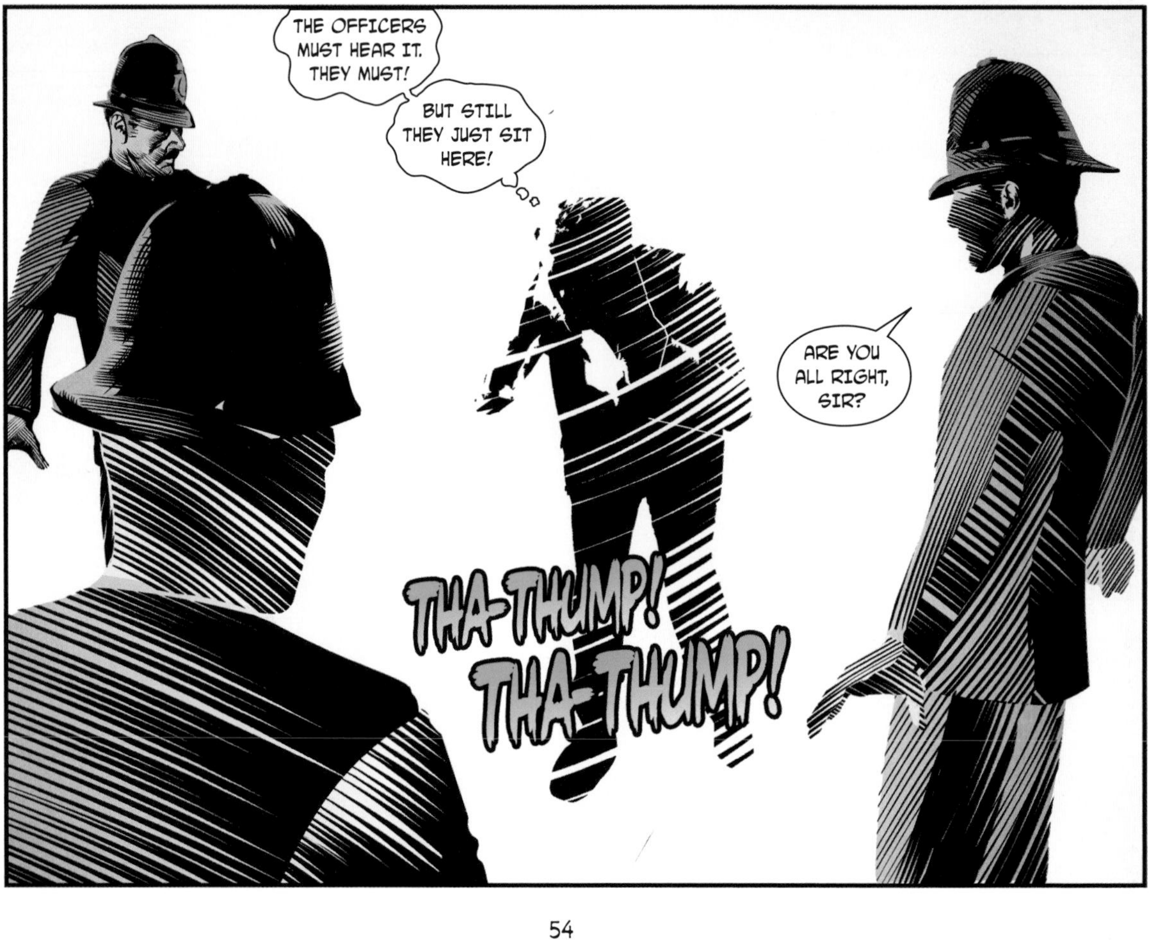
THE OFFICERS MUST HEAR IT. THEY MUST!
BUT STILL THEY JUST SIT HERE!
ARE YOU ALL RIGHT, SIR?
THA-THUMP! THA-THUMP!

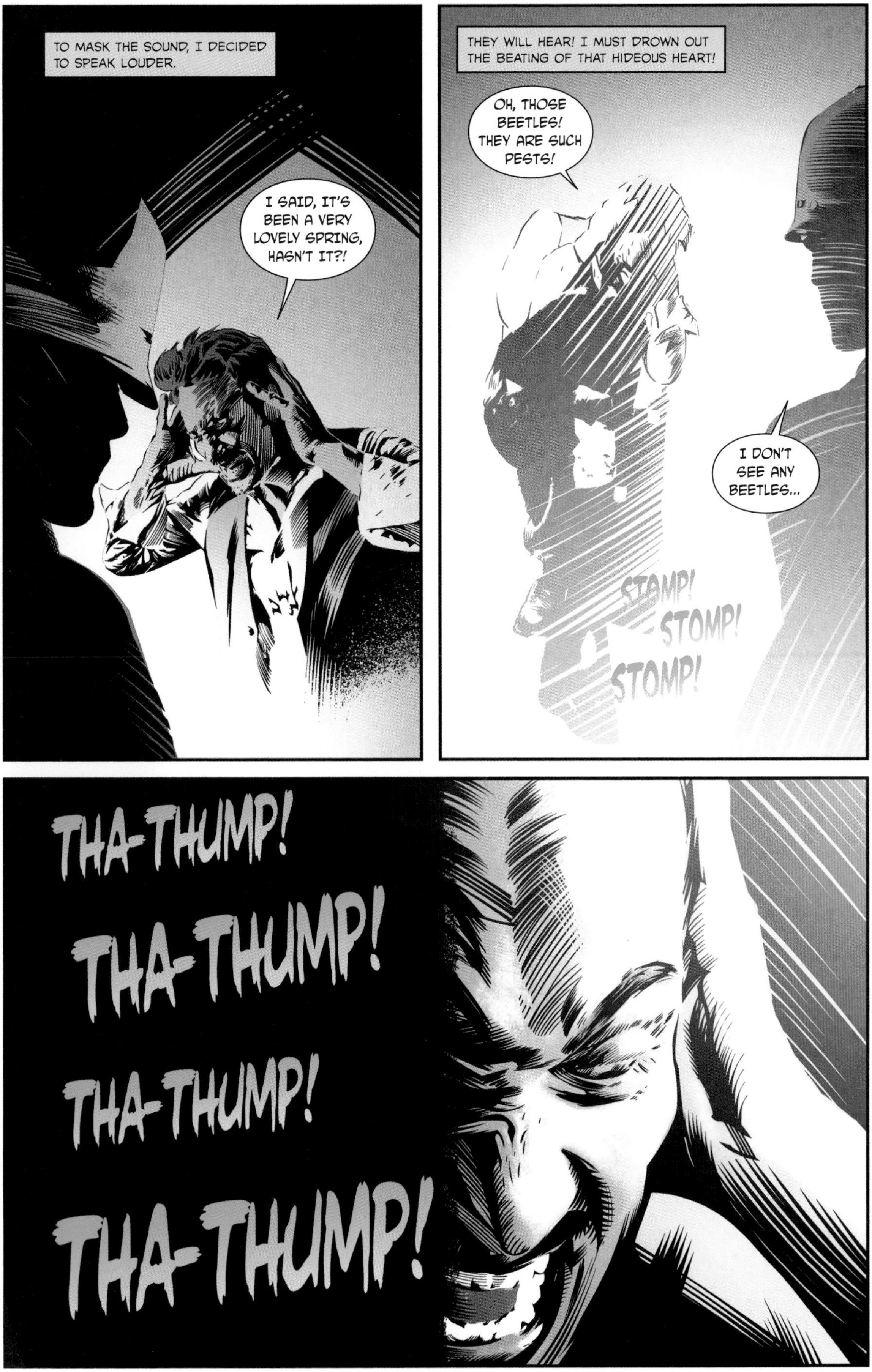
TO MASK THE SOUND, I DECIDED TO SPEAK LOUDER.
I SAID, IT'S BEEN A VERY LOVELY SPRING, HASN'T IT?!
THEY WILL HEAR! I MUST DROWN OUT THE BEATING OF THAT HIDEOUS HEART!
OH, THOSE BEETLES! THEY ARE SUCH PESTS!
I DON'T SEE ANY BEETLES...
STOMP!
STOMP!
STOMP!
THA-THUMP!
THA-THUMP!
THA-THUMP!
THA-THUMP!

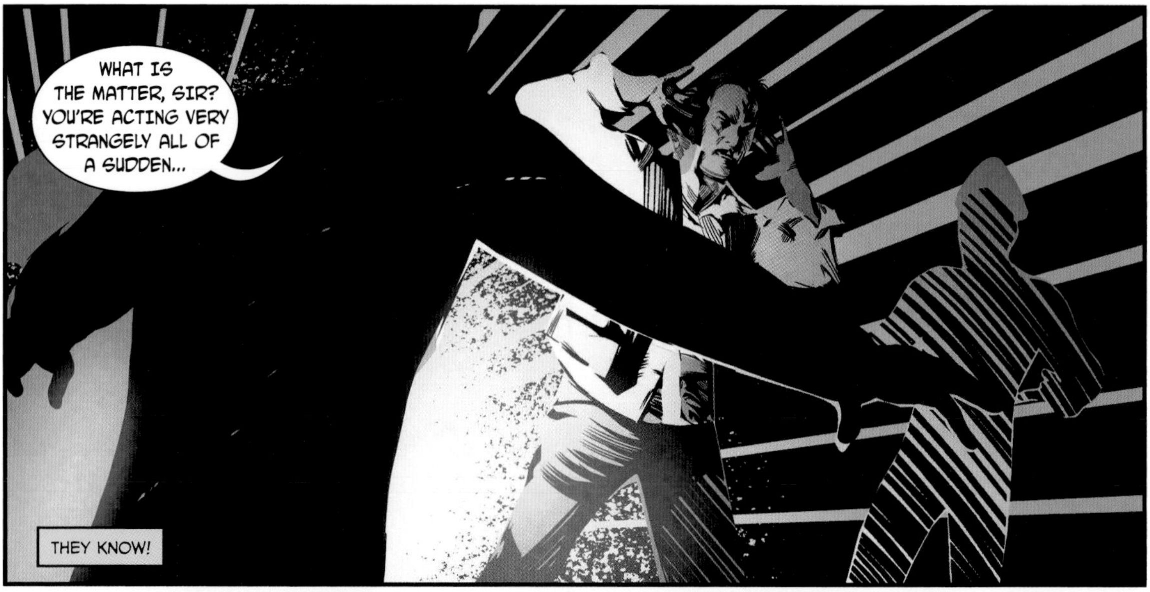
WHAT IS THE MATTER, SIR? YOU'RE ACTING VERY STRANGELY ALL OF A SUDDEN...
THEY KNOW!

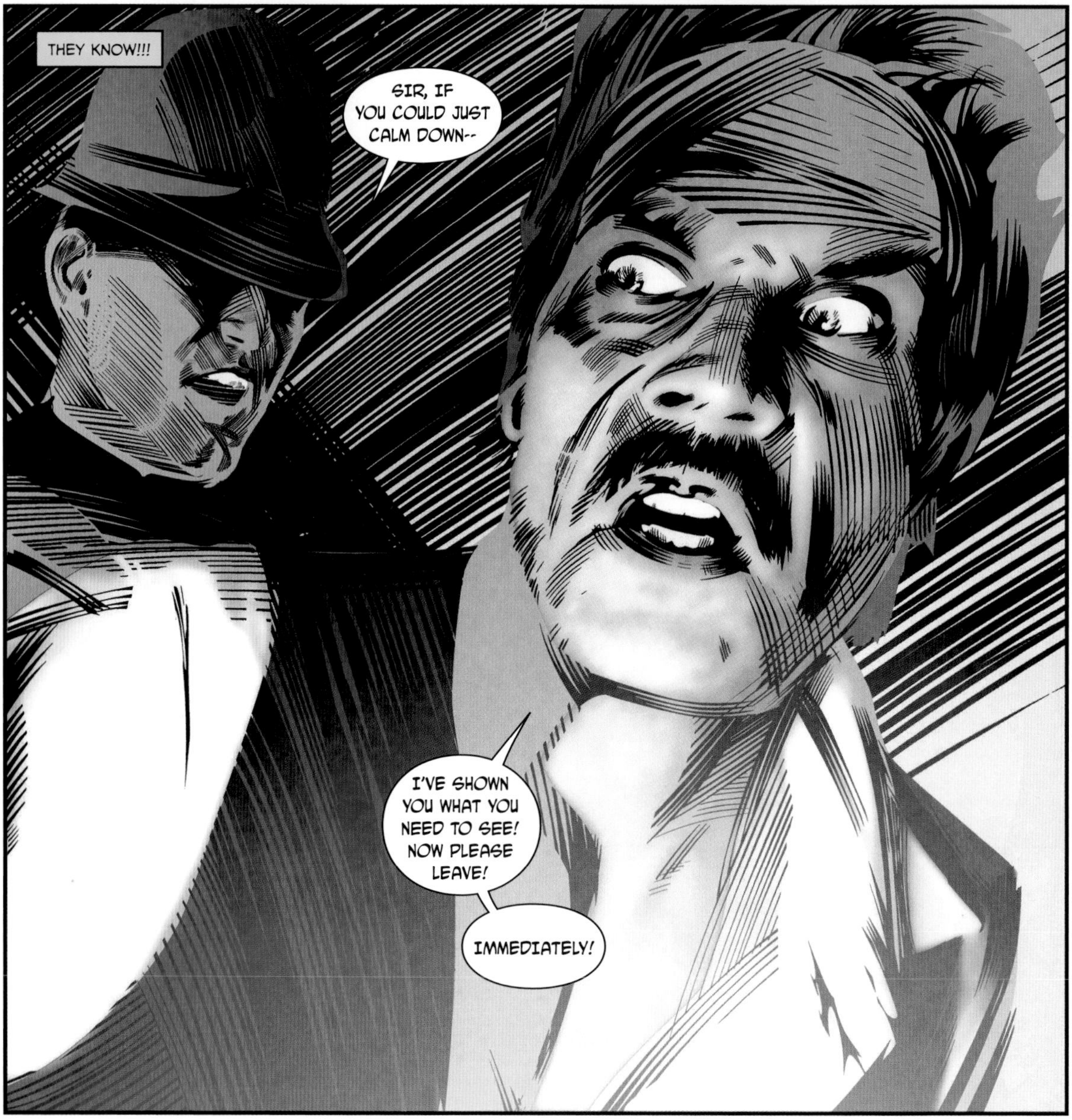
THEY KNOW!!!
SIR, IF YOU COULD JUST CALM DOWN--
I'VE SHOWN YOU WHAT YOU NEED TO SEE! NOW PLEASE LEAVE!
IMMEDIATELY!

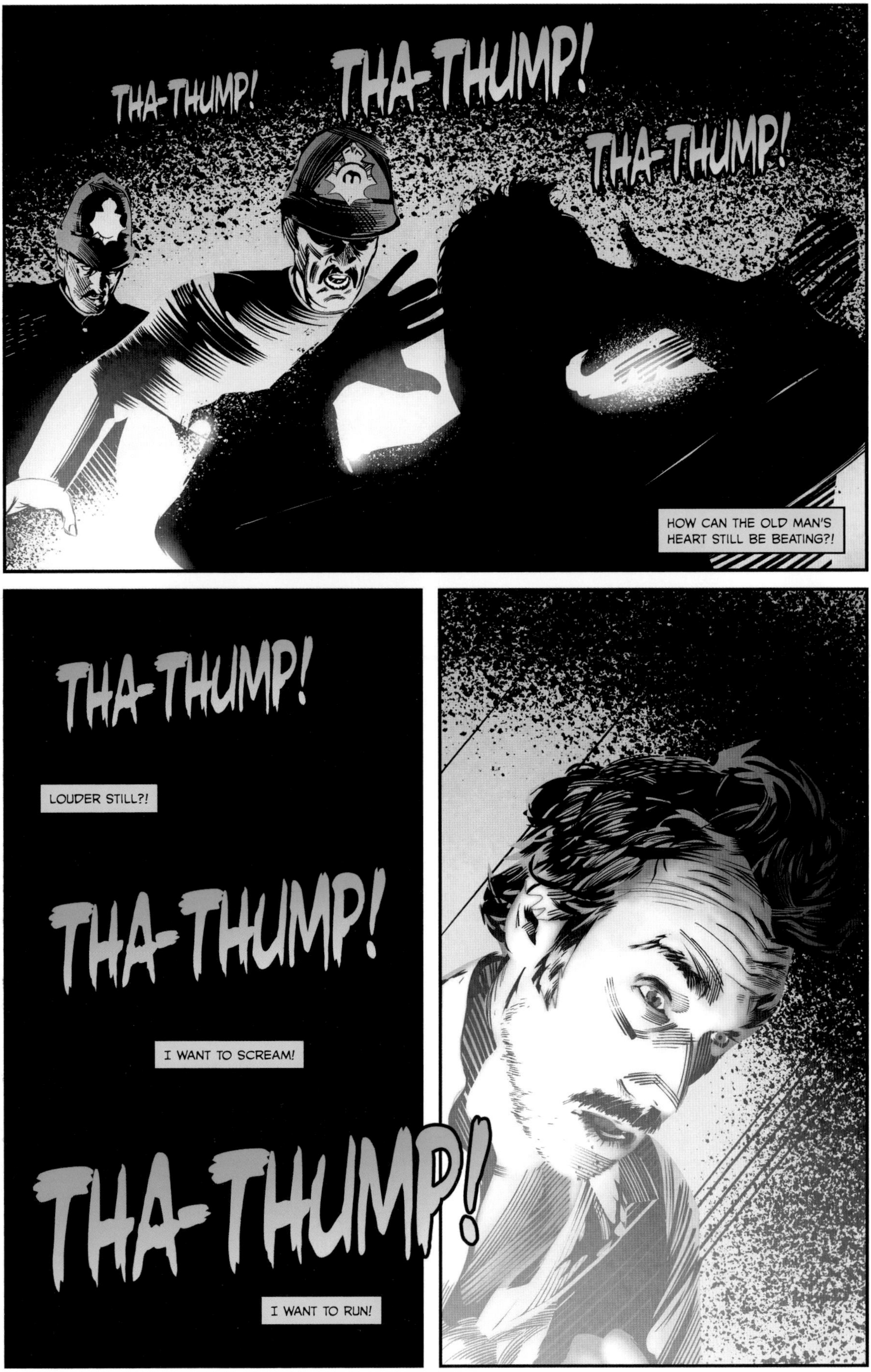
THA-THUMP!
THA-THUMP!
THA-THUMP!
HOW CAN THE OLD MAN'S HEART STILL BE BEATING?!
THA-THUMP!
LOUDER STILL?!
THA-THUMP!
I WANT TO SCREAM!
THA-THUMP!
I WANT TO RUN!

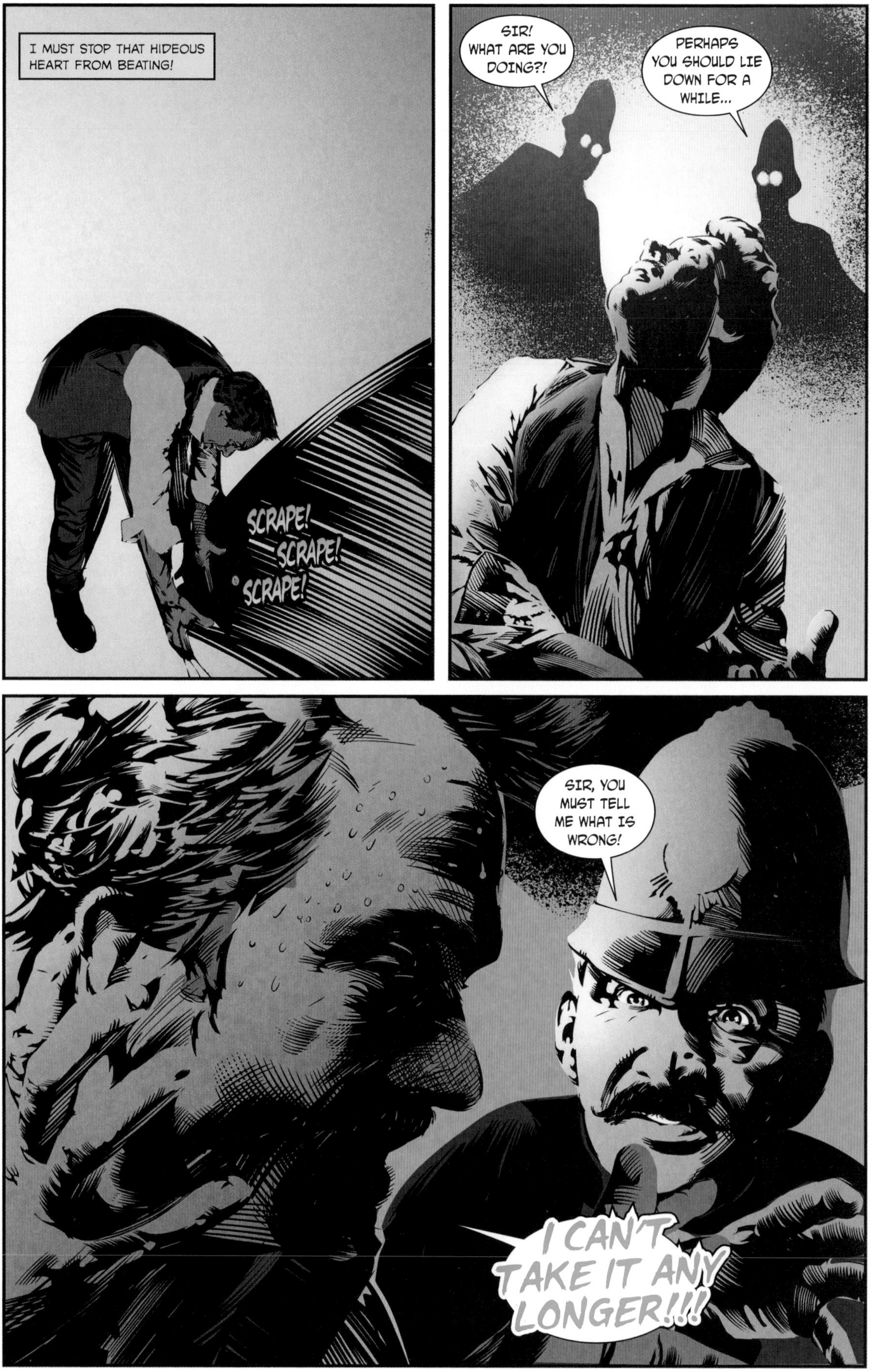

I MUST STOP THAT HIDEOUS HEART FROM BEATING!
SCRAPE!
SCRAPE!
SCRAPE!
SIR! WHAT ARE YOU DOING?!
PERHAPS YOU SHOULD LIE DOWN FOR A WHILE...
SIR, YOU MUST TELL ME WHAT IS WRONG!
I CAN'T TAKE IT ANY LONGER!!!

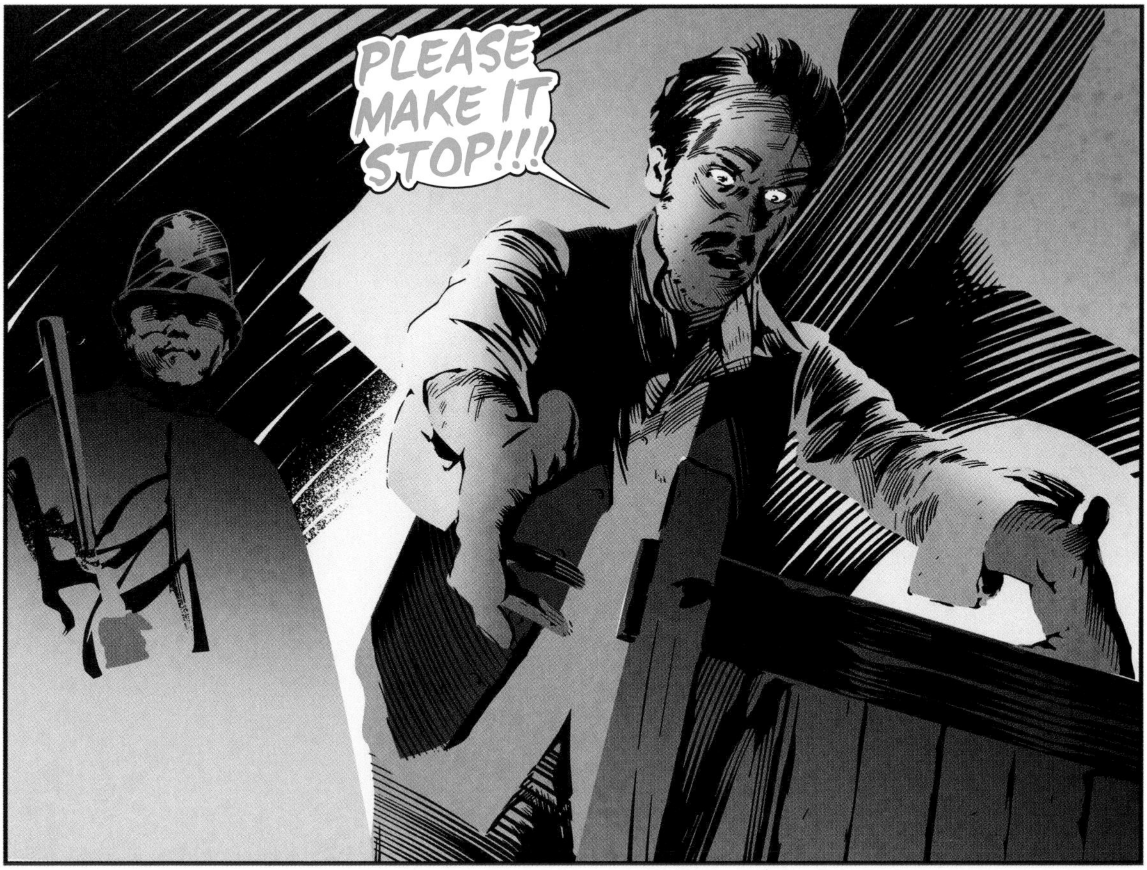
PLEASE MAKE IT STOP!!!

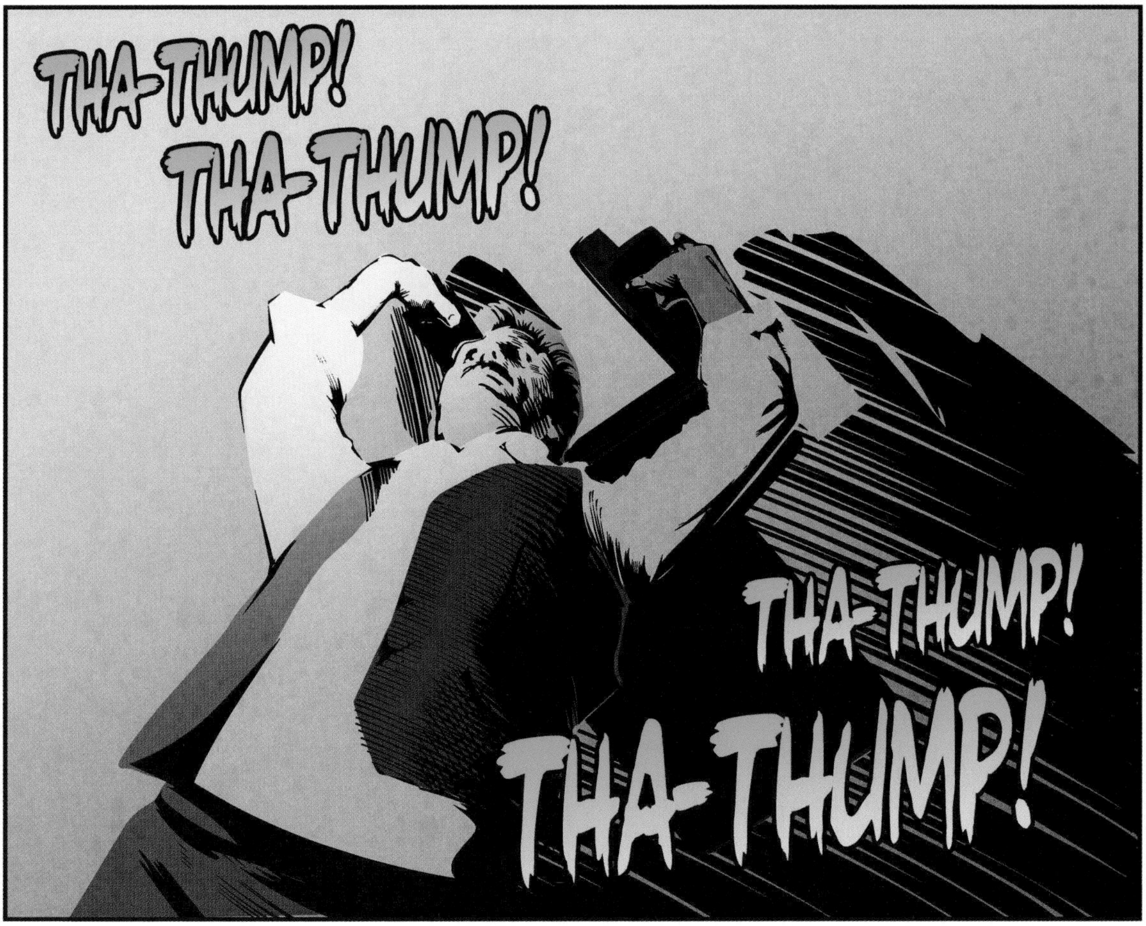
THA-THUMP!
THA-THUMP!
THA-THUMP!
THA-THUMP!

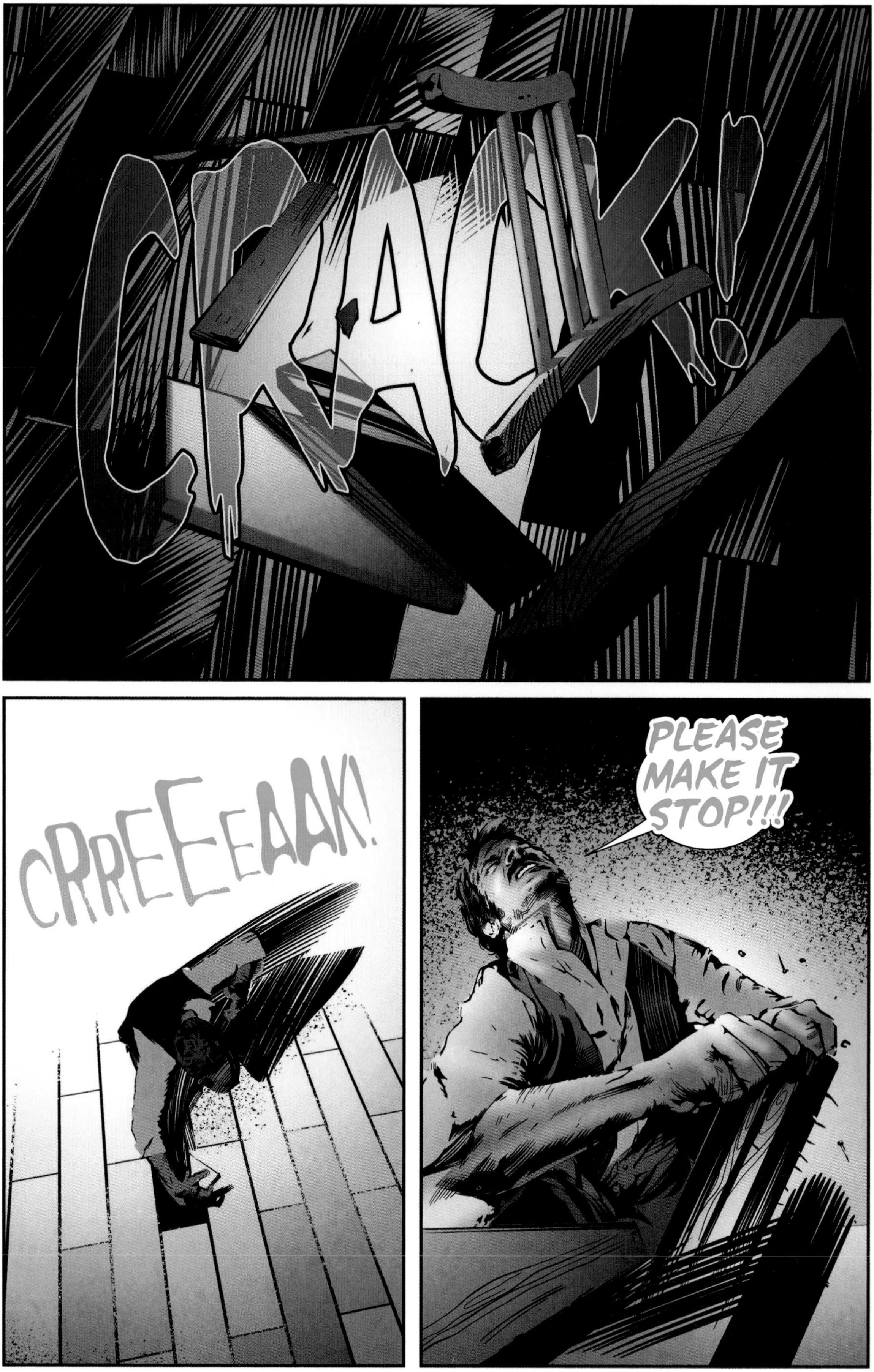
CRACK!
CRREEEAAK!
PLEASE MAKE IT STOP!!!

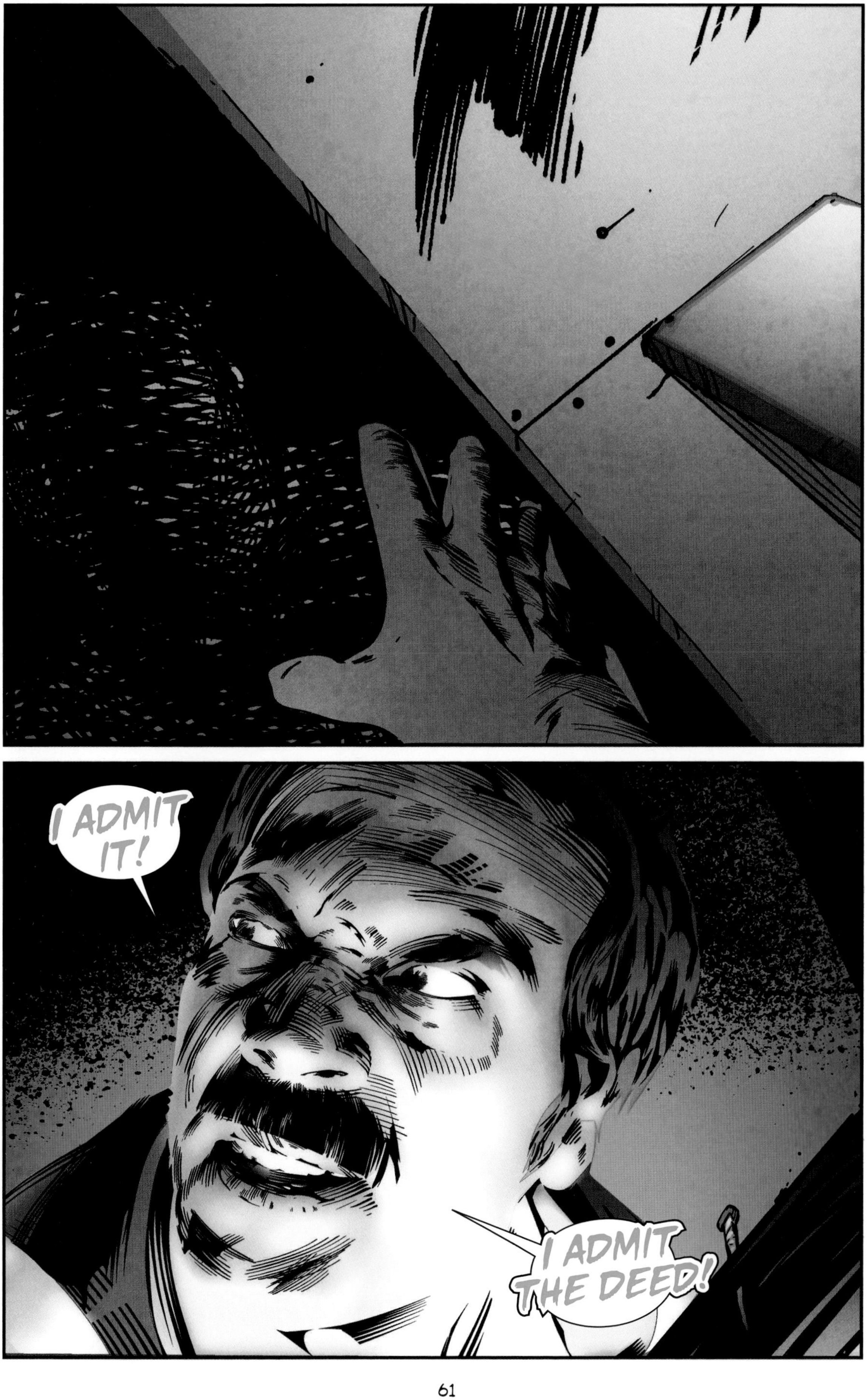
I ADMIT IT!
I ADMIT THE DEED!

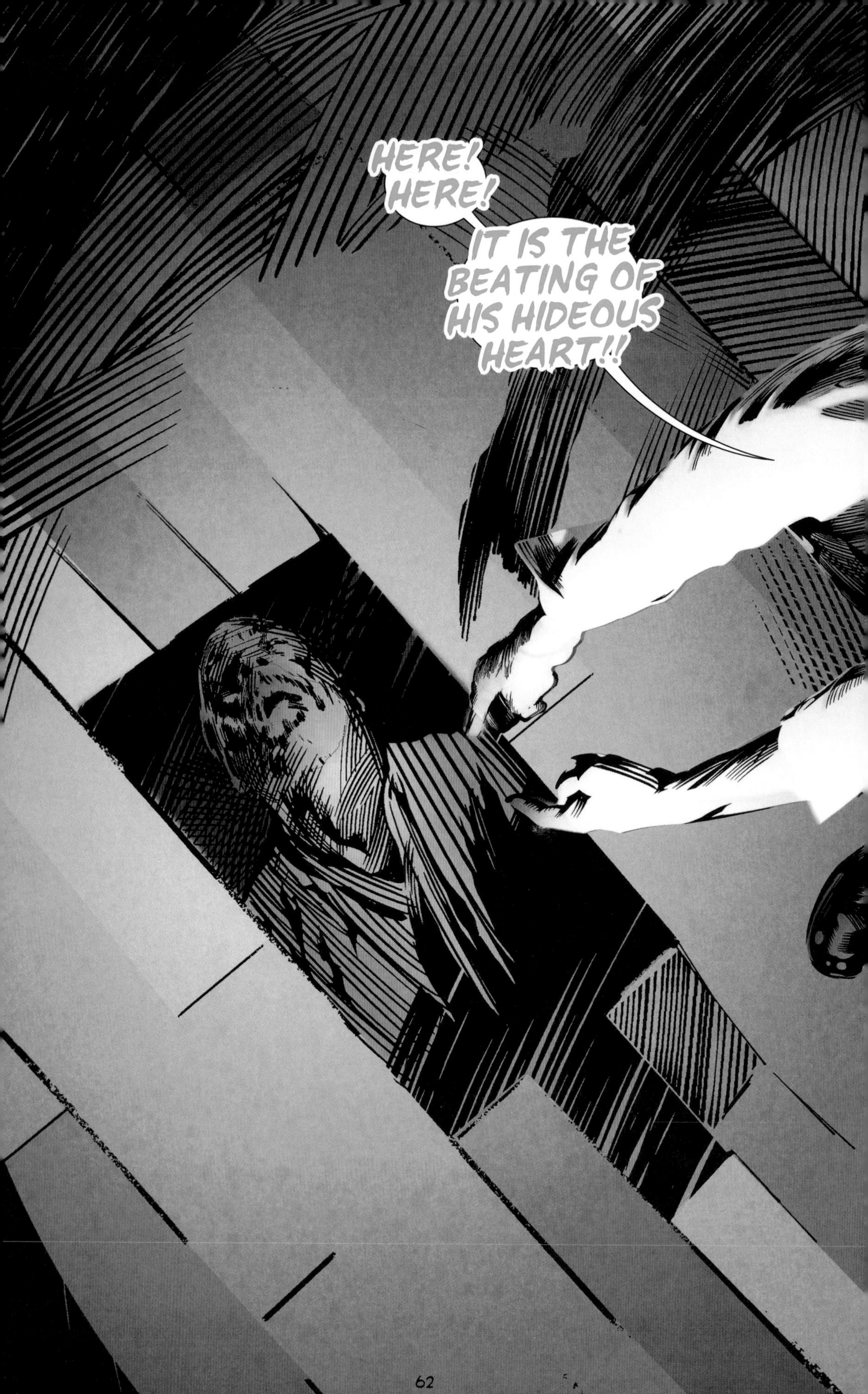
HERE! HERE!
IT IS THE BEATING OF HIS HIDEOUS HEART!!

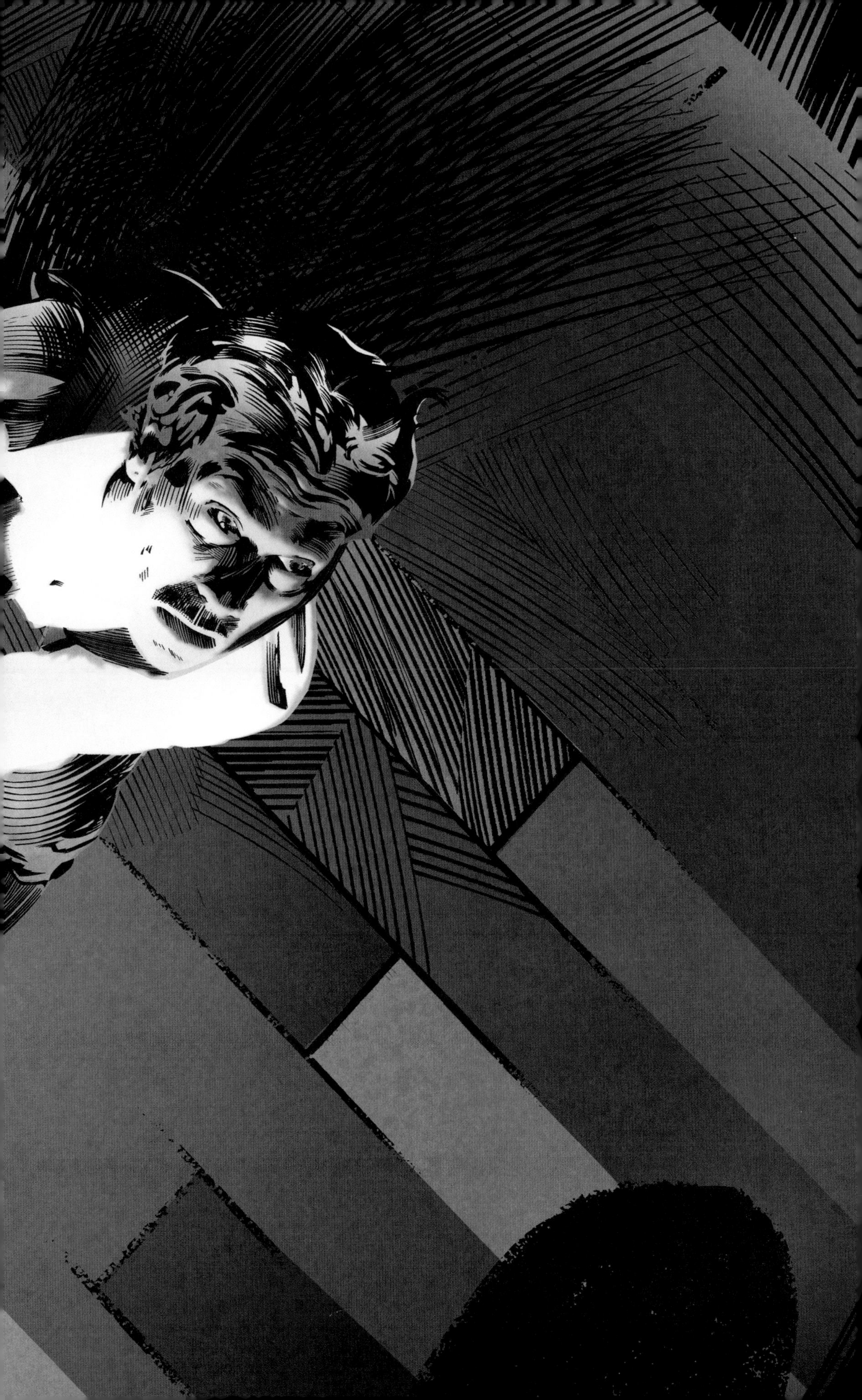

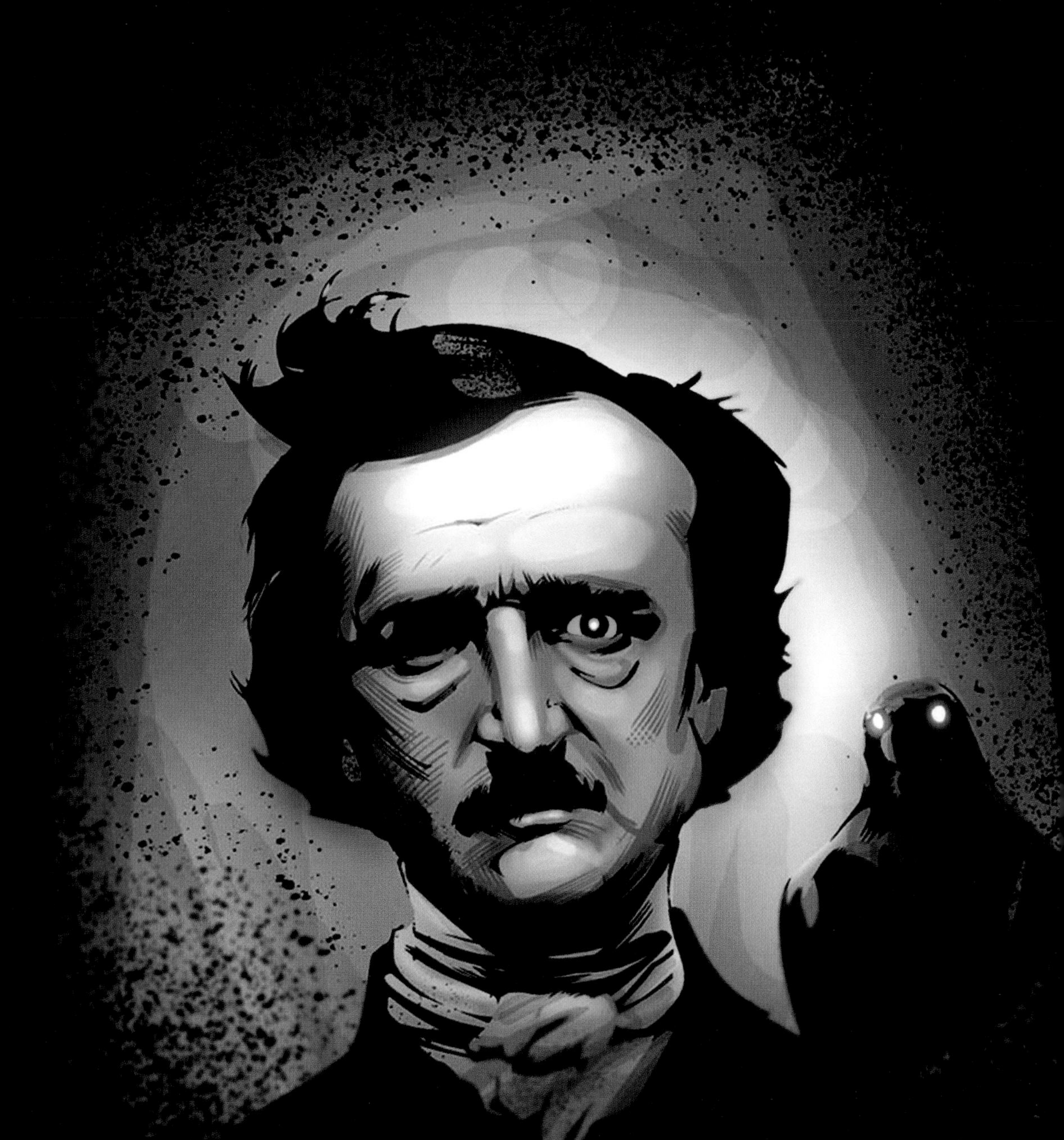

Over the course of his life, Edgar Allan Poe submitted many stories and poems to a number of publications. All of them were either rejected, or he received little to no compensation for them. His most popular work, "The Raven", quite nearly made him a household name——but only earned him nine dollars.

Poe was unable to hold a single job for very long, jumping from position to position for most of his life. He had very few friends, was in constant financial trouble, and struggled with alcoholism throughout his adult years. Edgar's family rarely helped him during these difficult times. In fact, when Edgar's father died in 1834, he did not even mention Edgar in his will.

Though largely unappreciated in his own lifetime, Edgar Allan Poe is now recognized as one of the most important writers of American literature.

THE RETELLING AUTHOR

Benjamin Harper has worked as an editor at Lucasfilm LTD., and at DC Comics. He currently works at Warner Bros. Consumer Products in Burbank, California. He has written many books, including *Obsessed With Star Wars* and *Thank You, Superman!*

THE ILLUSTRATOR

Dennis Calero is the award-winning artist of Marvel Comics' *X-Men Noir* and *X-Factor*, and the Capstone books *Frankenstein* and *The Invisible Man*. He was educated at Pratt Institute in Brooklyn, New York.

GLOSSARY

calculating (KAL-kyuh-lay-ting)--a calculating person schemes to make sure things work out the way he or she wants

cautious (KAW-shuhss)--if you are cautious, you try hard to avoid mistakes or danger

clever (KLEV-ur)--able to understand things or do things quickly and easily, or intelligently and carefully thought out

death watch beetle (DETH WOCH BEE-tuhl)--beetles that make a ticking sound as they bore through wood. The sound was once believed to be an omen of death.

deception (di-SEP-shuhn)--a trick that makes people believe something that is not true; a lie

evidence (EV-uh-duhnss)--information and facts that help prove something or make you believe that something is true

paranoid (pare-uh-NOYD)--baselessly suspicious of someone else's motives

peer (PEER)--to look hard at something that is difficult to see

perception (per-SEP-shuhn)--awareness of something through the senses, especially through sight or hearing

repulsive (ri-PUHL-siv)--very distasteful or disgusting

torment (TOR-ment)--great pain or suffering

VISUAL QUESTIONS

1. The creators of this comic chose to add a spotlight to the Narrator in some of the panels. Why do you think they chose to use the spotlight in some panels, but not others?

2. The main character is an unreliable narrator, or someone who cannot be trusted in a story told from his or her perspective. Identify a few instances in this book where the Narrator either lies, twists the truth, or seems to be imagining things.

3. In the left panel, we see the Narrator's eye. In the right panel, we see the Old Man's eye. Why do you think the creators of this comic chose to mirror their faces next to each other [on pages 22 and 23]?

4. The death watch beetles appear twice in this story. They are wood-boring insects known for making clicking sounds, and are sometimes considered to be symbols of death. Why do you think the beetles show up in the panels they do? [Pages 15 and 28.]

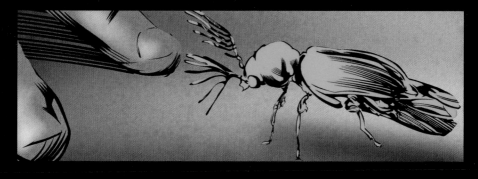

5. Based on the information given by the Narrator in the story, he and the Old Man have known each other for a long time. Are they friends? Coworkers? Father and son? Explain your answer using examples from the story.

INTRODUCING ANOTHER POE GRAPHIC NOVEL...

THE MURDERS IN THE RUE MORGUE

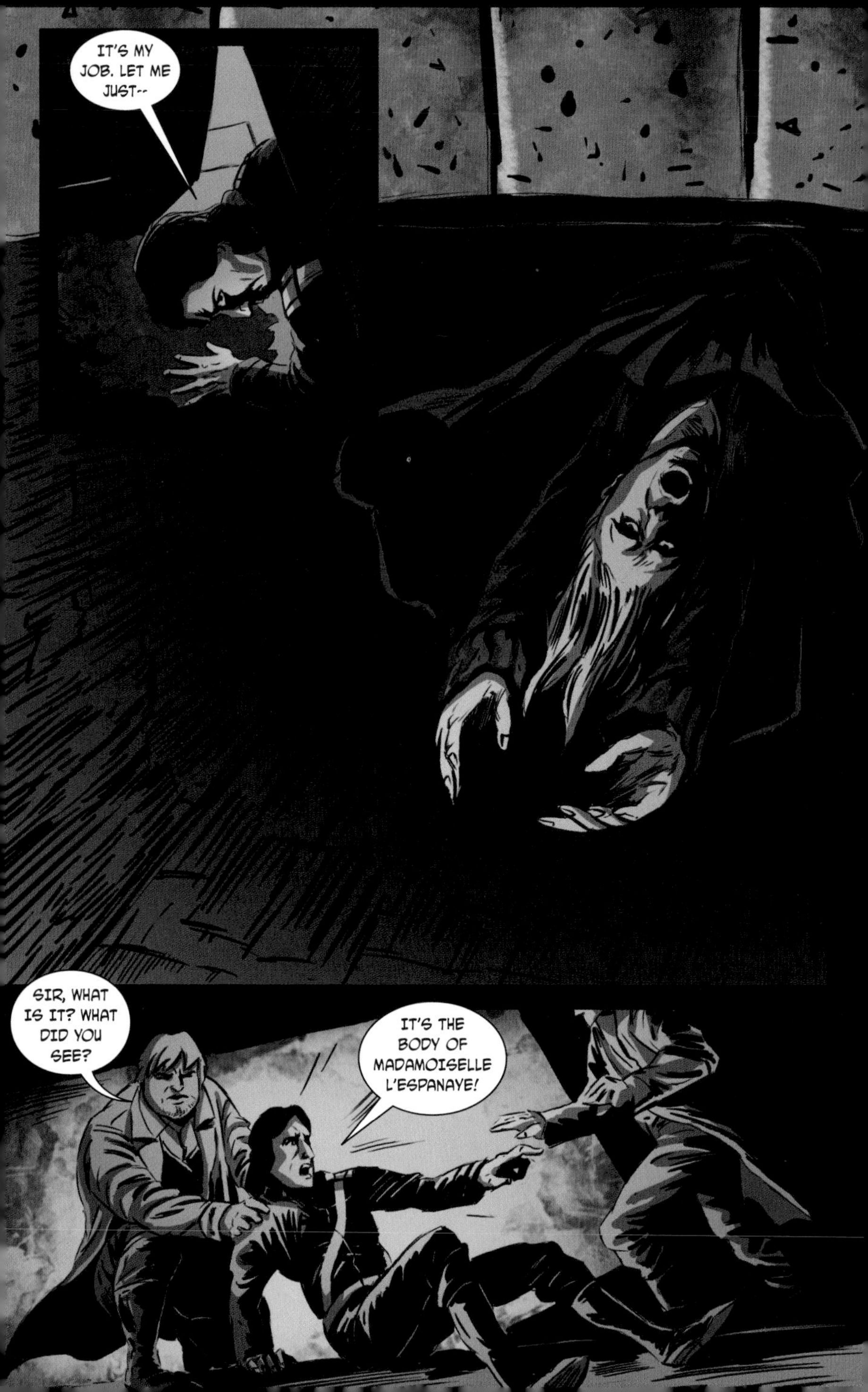

IT'S MY JOB. LET ME JUST--
SIR, WHAT IS IT? WHAT DID YOU SEE?
IT'S THE BODY OF MADAMOISELLE L'ESPANAYE!

Read all four

EDGAR ALLAN POE

graphic novels...

EDGAR ALLAN POE

THE TELL-TALE HEART

HARPER · CALERO

EDGAR ALLAN POE

THE FALL OF THE HOUSE OF USHER

MANNING · JIMENZ

EDGAR ALLAN POE

THE PIT AND THE PENDULUM

TULIEN · FABUL

EDGAR ALLAN POE

THE MURDERS IN THE RUE MORGUE

BOWEN · DIMAYA

ONLY FROM CAPSTONE

WWW.CAPSTONEPUB.COM

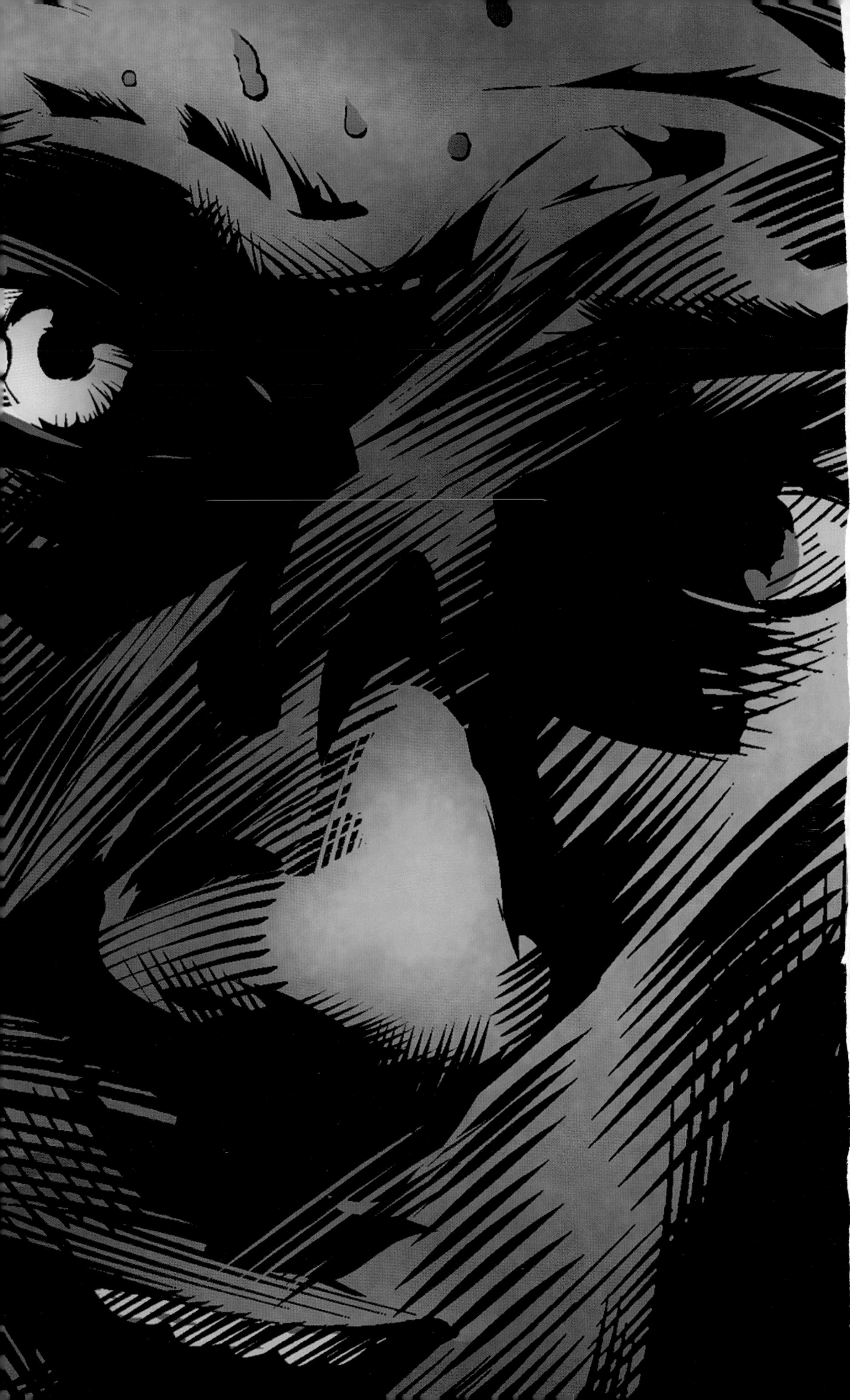